Cuban Heel

Leopold Borstinski

January 1952

1

"WHAT I LOVE about America is that the sidewalks are paved with gold."

"That's what I was told when I first arrived in New York, but the reality is different, Mr. President."

Alex Cohen and Meyer Lansky, members of the organized crime elite, sat with Carlos Socarrás, the Cuban president, as they sipped coffee and compared notes on the differences between their two great nations.

"I have seen the photographs, Alex, the walkways are so hot that the gold melts. I saw the steam, so it must be true."

Alex glanced at Meyer, who maintained his fixed grin and stared at this excuse of a man before him.

"Maybe it's in Harlem. I spent little time up there…"

The conversation continued in its stilted fashion for another five minutes before Meyer allowed it to slide away from the painful small talk and on to more important matters.

"I appreciate you are a very busy man, so I will get straight to it, if I may?"

A presidential nod indicated Socarrás was bored with pretending to care about the lives of the other people in his office.

"Cuba is a fabulous country, but it is on the cusp of becoming a great nation."

"There is no need to flatter me, Meyer. The people of my land have been neglected for far too long. They are impoverished, tired, and hungry. I hope that I may find some ways to ease their lot during my time in office."

"And we think we can help you with that. I will not pretend that we'll wave a magic wand and fix the difficulties you have here, but we offer a route for a sustainable revenue stream in the long term with the opportunity to secure foreign investment now and in the future."

Socarrás leaned back in his velvety chair and mulled this thought around his head as he inhaled deeply on his cigar.

"Fine words, Meyer, but what is it you are proposing?"

"I don't need to remind you that Havana is a quick plane ride away from Florida, which means we have an opportunity to encourage Americans to fly over here and spend their hard-earned wages."

"By any chance, do you have an idea what would attract those flies to travel to this midden?"

"Gambling. Alex and I created modern Las Vegas, which was nothing more than a desert town before we built casino-hotels and watched the money roll in."

Alex was surprised that Meyer had omitted the work by Benny Siegel, the real creator of gaming Vegas, but the fella was in full sales pitch and not concerned with historical accuracy.

"Mr. President, we can make the same thing happen here. Build casinos and other sources of entertainment to attract American tourists to spend US dollars—with your approval, of course."

Meyer sat back on the couch and gave Socarrás time to ponder the proposal. Alex couldn't tell if the guy was counting greenbacks in his mind or was concerned about the impact of American culture on this perfect isle.

"Foreign currency always interests the president."

"Inward capital flows are healthy for a country."

"I was speaking personally, but what is good for the president is good for the people."

"The investors I represent would want to build several casinos. The model would be to replicate what we have already achieved in

Nevada, only with less scrutiny of our day-to-day operations from the authorities."

"Meyer, I understand your situation. The American government has tried to shut down or curtail your business activities in Las Vegas several times, and you want to be left in peace. You see Cuba as the place where you can make your money without hindrance."

"More or less, yes."

"But I still represent a government and the Cuban state needs to be compensated for allowing you the freedom you seek."

"Mr. President, we would want to pay our taxes and contribute to the fabric of this nation. All we ask in return is that we are not hampered by excessive regulation or undue scrutiny of what we do within the casinos themselves. We need to be left alone to make our money."

"Exactly, so, I am sure you will have outgoings too and wish to have a level of privacy around the payments you make."

Meyer nodded and leaned forward, elbows resting on his knees.

"There is also the matter of how we show our appreciation to you for facilitating these arrangements."

"Half a million US dollars in small denominations, no consecutive serial numbers delivered to an address of my choosing before I lift a single finger to help you gentlemen destroy the moral fabric of my country."

BACK IN MEYER'S suite at the Hotel Nacional de Cuba, the two men discussed the morning's events. Meyer had been the underworld's financier for decades and funded the operations of organized crime across the United States. He did business with the Italian Mafia, the Irish, the Jews. Meyer didn't care who you were, where you came from, or how you earned your money, provided you paid what you owed when you said you would.

Alex was also a syndicate member, but he earned his money through hard work and a steely resolve. They had worked together since the start of Prohibition and Alex had dispatched Meyer's close friend, Benny Siegel, and a catalog of other known and less well-known figures.

"I like a man who knows his price."

"Meyer, the president had a figure in his head and was keen to ensure we got the message loud and clear. Does that mean we can trust him?"

"Alex, to be honest, I had a better feel for his predecessor, Batista, but the people voted the general out of office."

"That's politics, Meyer."

"That, my friend, is not putting enough money in the hands of the right officials on polling night. I have visited this place regularly since the war and the one thing you can be sure of is that everyone has a price and most will take at least ten percent less than it."

"So it is like doing business in America, only with a Spanish accent."

"Funny, Alex. If the president wants half a mill' then that is what it will cost to get our piece of Vegas in Havana. Only on this occasion, we can make sure our interests are put first and not our Italian friends."

"Not even Charlie Lucky?"

"He won't be leaving Sicily any time soon, which means other members of the mob are vying for the top job. Charlie's influence is waning and we must both accept that."

"Will you wire him the money, then?"

"There are elections in a few months and this president might not be around much longer. I'd prefer to wait and see who sits on the other side of the table once all the votes have been counted."

"A true democrat."

"I just don't wish to waste a bribe on that man."

"Why have the meeting now, Meyer?"

"Because you've only recently arrived in town and I want you to meet all the players. Besides, the promise of that much money in a private bank account might be the motivation our illustrious president needs to make sure he rigs the election his way."

2

ALEX HAD ONLY just arrived in Havana before meeting Socarrás, having used the opportunity since returning to the syndicate to further his interests in Las Vegas and extend the Trans-American racing news wire across the country. In those two years, he felt as though he had not spent any time with Sarah and was looking forward to being with her while they remained in Cuba.

"Have you any idea how long we're going to be on the island?"

"Can't say, hon'. It might be a few weeks or months, maybe longer."

"I asked Meyer the same thing, and he was as noncommittal."

"At least you know that when we tell you we have no clue, we mean it."

The couple sat on a veranda overlooking the city and tried not to guzzle their fruit cocktails. This was a country that enjoyed mixing its drinks, and Alex wondered if this was so they could hide how much they were cutting the alcohol. Then he remembered he was a far cry away from the blind pigs he used to supply during Prohibition.

"Alex, you know we haven't been on vacation since our trip here just after they brought you back into the syndicate?"

"Yes, sorry. Running Vegas took more of my time than when I was strong-arming johns who were chiseling the house."

"It wasn't a complaint, more of an observation."

"Sarah, do you think I'm reverting to my old ways like when we were married?"

"Oh no, Alex. Almost every weekend you've flown over to Jersey to visit me. You would never have done that before. I couldn't face the thought of living in Vegas and you have been very accommodating."

"I want you to be happy and also I understood you needed to be near New York to help run Meyer's office."

"That as well. He expects you to be on call day and night."

"Tell me about it. I've been with him for… thirty years now."

Alex knocked back the rest of his banana daiquiri and waited for the liquid to settle at the base of his stomach.

"Meyer has allowed us the weekend to be tourists before he sets you to work on Monday. Where would you like to go?"

"Show me the entire island, Alex."

"I've been inside a couple of hotels so far and not much else. So, we can discover the sights together."

THE NEXT MORNING, they hired a car and drove the two hours to reach Varadero, Cuba's second-biggest city, east of Havana.

"Remind me why we've come here, Alex?"

"Years ago, my friend Alfonse told me he had an enjoyable vacation here, so I thought we should check it out."

"If it was good enough for Capone, it's good enough for me."

The crowds were quieter in Varadero, which was no surprise, and the couple wandered around a market before settling down in a *taverna* for a bite to eat.

"We never seem to see where people live, do we, Sarah?"

"Well, that's because we spend our time near the visitor areas and hotels. The locals' homes will be somewhere else."

"Do you fancy looking behind the tourist facade?"

"If you like. Why the sudden interest in the ordinary john?"

"Don't worry, I haven't developed a heart overnight. If we are going to run a string of hotels eventually, then we need to understand how we shall ship in our staff."

"Alex, you always have an eye on the prize."

"Keep telling yourself it's one of my better traits you fell in love with."

"I'll bear that in mind, although your kindness was one of the first things that drew me to you."

Alex raised an eyebrow and Sarah squeezed his hand.

"Let's see what kind of world your staff exist in."

AS ALEX DROVE out of Varadero, there was a sudden falloff in the quality of the housing and the surface of the road. He had noticed it on the way into the city, but by heading south and avoiding the main artery to Havana, the effect was accentuated.

Instead of solid brick structures, walls and ceilings were made of corrugated iron and the outskirts of the city appeared more like a shantytown. Sarah placed a hand on Alex's shoulder to give herself comfort because the sights before them were far from pleasant.

"Just drive through, will you?"

"Sure thing. This reminds me of Alabama—the deprivation is immense. Everyone here is living in such squalid conditions. Meanwhile, Socarrás is happy to take a half a million bribe for the sake of us building a casino or two. That man deserves to get a bullet between the eyes."

"Instead of letting your blood boil, let's go back to Havana, Alex."

"There's no justice in this world."

"Since when have you been concerned about justice, Alex?"

He was silent for a spell as he ruminated on Sarah's question.

"If you can then you do, but we got to help those who can't help themselves."

"Is that how you've lived your life?"

"Not at all, but when I needed help after the Great War, who was there to help me?"

Sarah's cheeks reddened in recognition of the time she spent tending to Alex until he could walk again.

"Are you going to overthrow the Cuban government?"

"There's an election soon—the people's will shall prevail."

MARCH 1952

3

ALEX AWOKE TO hear a rumble in the streets, and he wondered what the hell was happening. He got out of bed as Sarah opened her eyes.

"What's going on?"

He stood out on their balcony and saw a mass of soldiers on the sidewalks, on the road. Everywhere.

"The army's arrived."

She whipped on a dressing gown and planted herself next to him. Before she could say anything, the phone rang, and he went inside to answer it.

"Have you seen what's happening?"

"The army is on the march, Meyer. Do you know what they are doing?"

"Stay indoors and you two'll be safe. From what I've heard, Socarrás won't be president by nightfall."

"What do you mean?"

"We are witnessing a military coup. The dust will settle by the morning and then we can deal with the new leader."

"Some trumped-up general with medals and no sense?"

"Let's not be too quick to judge. As soon as it's safe, we'll meet up, but don't go out today. Understood?"

ALEX PACED AROUND the living room of their suite until Sarah couldn't take it anymore.

"Please sit down. It's been thirty minutes since you spoke with Meyer and the day won't happen any faster if you wear a hole in the flooring."

He stopped, shoved his hands in his pants pockets, and shrugged.

"I can't stand being cooped up in here and don't you find the noise from outside deeply unsettling?"

They both craned to listen through the closed balcony doors. The constant stomping of military boots on paving stones was impossible to ignore, and there was a continual drone of voices interspersed with occasional cheers from onlookers.

Alex sighed and slumped into an easy chair hoping somehow this would make the sounds disappear, but he was wrong. A minute later, he stood up and walked onto the balcony. Sarah looked up from her book as she sat on the bed and carried on reading. Then she sauntered over to be with her man.

"Are you worried that this coup will kill off Meyer's plans?"

"For sure, but Meyer sounded remarkably calm for a fella who was about to have his dreams beaten to a pulp."

"What does he know that you don't, Alex?"

"Many things, Sarah. He always uses his noodle and never his hands. How he has survived all these years given the circles he's in is astonishing."

"Not when you consider how much gelt he has made. Meyer throws gelt at any problem he has. If the price is right, you can get anyone to do anything for you."

Alex nodded as he thought about the litany of people he had killed for money in his life. Big names, unknown men, but there was invariably a roll of greenbacks at the end. The only time he hadn't been paid was in the Great War and even then he'd come back with a Purple Heart. His ears pricked up as the crowd on the streets roared once more.

"I've gotta get out of here."

"Don't be a fool, Alex. Just wait it out, like Meyer said."

He shook his head and strode for the door before Sarah could put herself between him and the exit. As he walked into the hotel corridor, she tried to grab his sleeve, but he was too fast and carried on striding to the elevator.

The lobby was packed with concerned guests as Alex wove his way through the crowd and headed to the entrance. The doorman put his palm on the handle but didn't open it and refused to budge.

"Let me out."

"I'm afraid that's not possible, sir. Look outside. You will not be safe there and I cannot allow you to pass."

"That is not your decision to make."

He seized the doorman's hand and yanked it away from the handle. Before the guy knew what happened, Alex stood on the sidewalk and closed the door behind him.

HE MIGHT NOT have known much Spanish, but you didn't need to be a native speaker to understand what the locals thought of him as they went by. The soldiers continued to march in the road, but the men and women waving them past took only a few moments to shout and jeer at Alex.

He stood there for no more than twenty seconds and looked down briefly in disgust to see that his jacket was damp with spit. A globule landed on his cheek and Alex's eyes darted everywhere to find the culprit but no-go. His right hand formed a fist and Alex wanted someone to hit. He gritted his teeth and searched for a likely candidate for a pummeling, but he had no desire to punch a woman in the face, and he did not know who had perpetrated the crime.

He considered his next move and, despite himself, he knew there was only one thing he could do as the sea of people in front of him pinned him to the wall. He sighed again, turned round, and returned to the confines of the hotel.

BY THE TIME the couple woke up the following morning, the streets were quiet and mostly empty. Room service delivered their breakfast, and they sat on the balcony while they ate.

"I think it best if we take you back to the States in case it gets more dangerous here, Sarah."

"Is that your way of telling me you are going to repeat your foolishness from yesterday and don't want me to see you doing it?"

"Not quite. You were right, and I was wrong. I told you that when I got back to the room. Despite Meyer's optimism, the chances of this being a bloodless coup are remote. I know how men think and their propensity for violence. I would rather you were out of harm's way —only for a short time. As soon as I judge it is safe, I want you with me. But if there is trouble and Meyer needs my help, then I can't have a corner of my mind haunted by the possibility of you getting hurt."

Sarah was silent for a spell as she stirred her coffee and ate her cinnamon swirl.

"You must promise me not to do anything stupid. I don't want to go to your funeral."

"That's a solemn vow. We live together, we love together…"

"And we die alone."

With the decision made, Alex went inside to place some calls and make the arrangements. The airport was open, although the army was restricting access to flights.

"Meyer, have you any influence to get Sarah over to Florida until the heat dies down?"

"I've already opened lines of dialog so safe passage shouldn't be too difficult to organize. Will you be going with her?"

"Yes, but only to make sure everything is all right. My plan is to turn tail and get the next flight back in."

"Returning will be easy. Flash some dollars and customs will lie down and beg. Getting out needs a quiet word in the right ear, which is exactly what I can do. I'll let you know when you are safe to leave. In the meantime, pack your things and wait. You'll be out of here before the evening."

Yet again, Alex paced up and down in the living room, waiting for a call from Meyer Lansky.

◆ ◆ ◆

WHEN ALEX AND Sarah landed in Miami, a fella with a black limousine greeted them and took them straight to a mansion on the edge of the city. Sam Giancana opened the door as they arrived.

"Thank you for helping us at such short notice, Sam."

"I am always happy to help a friend of Meyer's and fellow syndicate member. And this must be Sarah. Good to meet you."

"Meyer has spoken highly of you over the years."

"Pleased to hear it. Do you know him well?"

The confusion on Sam's face reflected his assumption that she was Alex's skirt.

"Sam, I have been his executive assistant for a decade, more or less."

"And to make matters more complicated, Sarah and I were divorced before I first went out to Vegas but reconnected two years ago, around when I got back into the syndicate after the Kefauver hearings."

By the time the story of their lives was complete, the three had sauntered into the house and sat in a living room.

"Would you like to freshen up, Sarah?"

"Thanks, Sam, but there's no need to worry on my account."

He nodded but said nothing, staring at Alex and creating an uncomfortable silence until Sarah tutted, asked for the bathroom, and left the room.

"How are things in Havana, Alex?"

"The military swept into power yesterday, so who knows what is going on. Meyer is optimistic; he probably funded the coup, knowing him."

"I couldn't say. What's important to me is that the potential to entice American tourists over there remains undiminished."

"Too early to determine. I don't know who, if anyone, is in charge, let alone what their response will be to foreign money. In a week or two, we'll see. Meyer is staying put, so I'd guess it'll be all right. He hasn't made a poor investment yet."

"Alex, even the Flamingo turned a profit in the end."

"With and without Benny's help."

Sarah returned and Sam stopped talking.

"Sam, please discuss matters in front of Sarah. She knows Meyer's business inside out and appreciates the importance of omertà."

"Apologies, Sarah. I am not used to conducting business in front of women."

Sam offered Sarah the use of a guest cottage in his grounds, and Alex stayed long enough for a bite to eat before heading back to Havana.

4

THE NEXT DAY, Alex met up with Lansky as the coup had all but fizzled out. The army was in charge, and Cuba's citizenry was being encouraged to remain indoors when they weren't going about their lawful business.

"Great to see you, Meyer. How has the place been in my absence?"

"Calming down. You were right to want to get Sarah away, but the new president has done a good job of protecting American tourists from any angry locals."

"Sounds quite open-minded, not like one of those fascists who were running around Europe."

"Not at all."

There was a glint in Meyer's eye that meant Alex couldn't decide whether he was being serious.

"Do you think we can carry on doing business with these army guys, Meyer?"

"I never deal with soldiers. I'm always more interested in speaking with the organ grinder and not a bunch of monkeys."

"Is there an obvious leader in the armed forces?"

"It's most unlike you not to read the morning papers, Alex. I'm surprised you haven't heard that Batista kicked all this off."

Alex stopped for a second to take stock.

"The same guy who you were schmoozing when Benny was still alive?"

"One and the same. He didn't like losing the popular vote a few years ago and figured the best way to make sure he became top dog again was to seize power before the next election. It saves on all the effort of counting votes and declaring winners."

"How long have you known Batista was behind all this?"

"Alex, where do you think he got the money to afford to take over the country in the first place?"

"Sometimes, I don't know why I am ever surprised about anything you do."

"Too kind. I like to make sure I have all bases covered, that's all."

WHAT LITTLE OPPOSITION there was, Batista crushed within a week, and he consented to an audience with Meyer and Alex almost immediately. The three sat in the same room occupied by his predecessor; the only significant difference was that Batista wore military dress instead of a suit. Alex wondered which of the medals gleaming on his chest he had earned and how many he'd added for effect.

"Thank you for taking the time to see us, Fulgencio."

"Meyer, you are most welcome as you know. I am glad I have been able to return my country to a leadership that will be strong and have the best interests of Cuba in his heart."

"Indeed. Let me introduce my business associate, Alex Cohen. He owns and runs several businesses in Las Vegas and has direct experience of the hotel and casino world. Given what we have already discussed, I thought you would both gain advantage by discussing the future of Havana."

"Very pleased to make your acquaintance, Mr. President."

"Meyer has spoken of you to me before. Your control of Las Vegas and your knowledge of gaming and other matters may prove highly lucrative for us all and beneficial to the humble people of Cuba."

"From what I have seen of your wonderful country so far, I am certain we can find more ways to lure American tourists over here to part with their greenbacks."

Batista laughed at this comment and Alex wondered how a powerful man like the general could have such a small head. A second glance showed him that the man's jacket had puffed up shoulder pads to create the illusion that he was bigger than he was.

"If you gentlemen are prepared to make appropriate investments, then I am sure we shall all prosper from your endeavors."

"Naturally, we will want to help you give the opportunity to enjoy this fabulous country to as many Americans as we can."

Alex listened and eased himself into his seat with every word Meyer spoke. This man before them didn't care about his people otherwise they wouldn't have been able to get to see him so early in his tenure. Lining his pockets was his highest priority no matter what he said.

The meeting continued with Meyer blowing smoke up Batista until there was nothing more to say. Alex recalled his days sat in oak-lined rooms in Tammany Hall when the Bowery was the extent of his world. Politicians were the same wherever they lived—fine words leave their lips, but it is their wallets that shape their thoughts and deeds.

As they walked out of the palace, Meyer turned to Alex.

"You should arrange for Sarah to come back. She'll be as safe here as in Sam's guest cottage, and there's much to accomplish."

"What's there to do? I didn't notice any deals being struck with Batista just now."

"We need to structure an offer to him that means we will take control of the gaming interests in Havana. That is going to require an amount of money and significant planning. With this trumped-up dictator in charge, we have got a green light to do whatever we want to establish a Cuban Las Vegas, but with none of the hassle from any local or federal authority. It's time to make some gelt."

MARCH 1955

5

"IT'S GREAT TO see you, David."

Alex looked at his son with admiration. The young man had made something of himself and could fund a trip to Havana.

"Likewise, Pop."

"How's business?"

"Good, thank you. Lawyers and funeral directors. Somebody always wants one or the other."

"And who wants to hang around dead bodies, right?"

"You should know, Pop."

Alex eyed David as he crossed his arms but let the comment slide even though he took offense at his son's words. Alex figured the kid wouldn't have traveled all this way just to get under his skin. Besides, he called David a kid but as Sarah reminded him, the guy was a man, from the set of his jaw to the clothes on his back. The puppy fat had long since been shed and a lean joe sat in front of him in the Cantina Lima Hastiada, a local bar around the corner from David's hotel.

"If you had called ahead, we would have been happy to let you stay with us."

"That's all right. I didn't know I was coming over until the day before and even then, I don't want to be a bother."

"How could that be? You are our flesh and blood."

"To be honest, Pop, I thought it might be hinky, what with you and Mom back together. It just did not feel right, and I can't live under my parents' roof anymore. At some point, you must let your children stand on their own two feet."

"Wise words. I'm glad your mother brought you up well."

"So am I."

They clinked their drinks—Alex's coffee and David's tequila—and continued to talk the afternoon away.

"Would you compromise your independent spirit by agreeing to eat with us this evening? I know Sarah would rather cook for you than hop to a restaurant. It's a mama's right."

"Of course. Please don't be offended, but I'm not sleeping under your roof."

"I'm teasing. I'd want to go out and party in this town if I was your age too. Shall we say seven, then?"

"Sure thing."

A hug and Alex left the cantina, although he gave instructions to the bar owner that David could continue to order without getting charged a peso.

FROM THE MOMENT Alex arrived back home to the minute David knocked on the door, Sarah filled her day with cooking, laying the table, and preening in the bedroom mirror. Alex couldn't remember the last time she'd seemed so concerned to make everything perfect unless he counted her preparation of Meyer's general ledger.

"It's been so long," she uttered as soon as her tears of joy had subsided enough for her to regain her breath. Alex shook David's hand and offered another hug.

"Can I make you a drink?"

"Only if you are having one."

Alex poured two Scotch on the rocks and a glass of red wine for Sarah, who finally sat down after scurrying in and out of the kitchen for the first five minutes.

"What did you get up to this afternoon, dear?"

"Nothing much. I spent most of the time sipping a coffee and watching the world go by outside the hotel."

"Oh, to have no responsibilities."

"I'm sure you could retire whenever you wanted to, Pop."

"Good to hear you have such faith in my past success, but if I could stop, I surely would."

"Whatever you say, Pop."

David glanced at Sarah whose eyebrows rose up her forehead and he thought he heard her molars grinding. Alex ignored the disbelief on her face.

"I've set a little aside so that your mother and I can look after ourselves when we get old, but don't hold your breath for any inherited fortune from me."

"That's not what I was angling for, Pop. The only money I want to spend is the gelt I have earned myself."

"Pleased to hear it and I may even take you at your word one day."

David inhaled as if to respond, and Alex pointed a finger at him.

"Gotcha."

They laughed, and the conversation continued in a lighter vein until Sarah announced she was ready to serve dinner.

AFTER DAVID HELPED his mother to clear the table, the three sat back down and took simple pleasure in their coffees. Alex stared at his son and his chest puffed up. Most of his memories of the children were from when they were toddlers. After that, he was absent from their lives—prison and living on the other side of the country does that to young minds.

"You never said how long you were going to be on vacation here."

"No, Pop. That's because I don't have a good answer."

"How so?" Sarah intervened almost without thinking, the words squeaked out for both men to hear.

"I am on sabbatical."

"What does that mean, son?"

"My firm has let me take a month or two off and I can return afterward."

"Why do you need such a long rest? Have they been working you into the ground?"

"Nothing like that, Mom. I've left on good terms."

Alex's ears pricked up.

"Are you on sabbatical or are you unemployed? There's a world of difference between the two."

"There sure is, Pop. Let me explain my situation and then you'll both be able to breathe again."

David shot a glance at Sarah, who didn't appear to have exhaled since she uttered her last words.

"I have been very successful at Bernstein and Bernstein. They have treated me well and I have learned a tremendous amount from them."

"And…"

"But the idea that I will spend the rest of my life helping corporations avoid tax fills me with dread."

"Accountants and undertakers, kid."

"Yeah, the thing is I want to give back."

"Work for a charity, you mean?"

"No, Mom, closer to home. You guys are cooking up some fantastic schemes here and I'll bet that the deals that are concocted will require a trained professional eye over them. And those eyes need to be ones you can trust, right?"

"If a deal is good enough for Meyer, it gets my seal of approval."

"I'm sure it does, but do you not think at some point your business partner might prioritize his own concerns over yours and Mom's?"

Alex sat back in his chair and mulled that thought over. He had never considered the possibility that his and Meyer's interests would be anything but aligned. The fella had looked after him since before he went to Sing Sing in '36.

"Suppose you are correct, David—and I'm not sure you are, mind—what are you proposing?"

"Let me come and work for you, Pop. When I look back on my time on this earth, the two people I owe everything to are sat at this table and I have done nothing to repay you."

"Apart from all the joy you and your brothers have brought me and your father over the years."

"Mom, a smile on your face doesn't pay to keep a roof over your head."

"Now you are sounding like Meyer—a true accountant. Besides, we didn't become parents for our children to pay us back. That's not how life works."

"I understand. I wish to work in the family business. I am sick and tired of making money for other people and want my kin to benefit from what I do."

Alex's back stiffened at David's words.

"Have you any idea what I do for a living?"

David laughed and nodded.

"When we were kids, we were regularly strafed with bullets in our bedrooms at night, so we had a pretty good sense before we reached double digits."

A heat in Alex's cheeks made him shuffle in his seat and he looked away from David for a moment.

"It happened once, to be fair to your father."

"True, but let's not forget that Arik was kidnapped, and he talked through every minute of the ordeal for us."

Alex's shoulders sagged, and he stared at his glass as he swilled his Scotch around. Sarah reached over and placed a hand on his arm, and his lips curled upward for a second before slumping on his face.

"Pop, I mention this not because I want to rub your nose in the past, but you need to understand that I know how you make your gelt and it isn't as a sales rep. Also, I am thirty-three and I've been able to read the newspapers for several years now. You forget you get mentioned almost every time some mobster gets killed on the streets of LA, Chicago, Las Vegas, or New York, and in places you've probably never even visited."

Alex exhaled and looked at Sarah before staring at his son. He saw her bite her lip and rock in her chair.

"David, let me think about your proposal for a while. Enjoy the sights and sounds of Havana and we'll talk in a few days. This is a big decision and I do not want to rush to any conclusion."

"IF YOU LET him into your affairs, you might as well sign his death warrant."

Sarah had waited until Alex drove David back to his hotel and the words burst out of her before Alex sat down in the living room.

"Sarah, he's a tax lawyer. The worst that might happen is that he is surprised by some of my financial affairs or gets a paper cut from a ledger. I will not ask him to take a bullet for me."

"Don't even joke about such things, Alex, but I am worried about him. We have spent his entire life trying to protect him from what you do and the life I left behind. Now he turns up at our door, demanding to be allowed into our dark world. And it is filled with the bad and the ugly. That's not what I want for our son."

"Nor me, Sarah. But it sounds like it is what David wants. If he were to come on board, then I would only involve him in my legitimate deals. Nothing that could link him to anything criminal."

"Don't you think that if he even touches our world then he will be tainted for the rest of his life?"

"The apple has already fallen from the tree and it hasn't landed very far, it would appear."

6

THE NEXT ORDER of business was to introduce David to Meyer before they met with President Batista. Alex had visited the same office many times over the previous couple of years. His comfort in the room was in marked contrast to David's response to the same furniture, and the general sat on the other side of his large oak-lined desk.

"Fulgencio, always good to see you, my friend."

Batista nodded and his medals jangled on his chest. Sometimes Alex couldn't look past those lumps of cheap metal and notice the guy behind the stern grimace.

"Meyer, there is nothing I enjoy more in this world than catching up with you and your business partners."

The head of state glanced at Alex with a flicker of acknowledgment and ventured a disdainful slit-eye for David. He had been alerted to who would be in attendance, so there was no need for this childish response to the man.

"President Batista, let me introduce my newly-appointed head of legal affairs, David Cohen."

"I see nepotism isn't the sole preserve of Latin American countries, it would appear."

"Yes, he is my son, but I employ him because he is a qualified lawyer with vast experience in international law."

"And so young with it."

Alex let Batista's comment fall to the floor unnoticed because the dictator wanted to score points, and Alex knew there were far more important matters at hand than winning an argument with this *farbissener momzer*.

Before they completed the preliminary pleasantries, another man entered the room and sat on a chair near Batista. "This is the Mayor of Havana, Francisco."

"Do I detect a family resemblance?"

"Yes you do, Alex. Francisco is my brother."

A quip about nepotism flashed through Alex's mind, but he let it go.

"We want to follow up on a conversation you and I have had several times over the years—investment in the entertainment sector in Cuba."

"Meyer, we both know that we just need to find the right way of working, and then we can both have our dream of a Latin Las Vegas become a reality. Last time we spoke, you said you would come back with a proposal."

"And that is why we are all in the room today. As a reminder to you and to ensure your brother is up to speed, the issue I face is that we require a considerable amount of money to build and maintain a casino and hotel complex before we realize any profit. This is millions of US dollars."

"We are aware of the scale of the investment needed."

"Then you understand that people who own those amounts of capital do not want to put it at risk before they can gain a return on their largesse. This means we need to have the right environment in which to place our investments."

"Environment?"

"Somewhere safe where the government will support our efforts and where we can rely on the local police force to protect our building and staff."

"You want us to guard your casinos?"

Batista raised a finger to quieten Francisco who had interrupted Meyer.

"I call for you to prevent any harm befalling my hotel, but this is not a free service. You have personal costs to cover and the local and national agencies must be supported too so that the wheels of commerce may turn."

"How much, Meyer?"

"If I were to make a payment to one of your Swiss bank accounts of, say, half a million, would that help us receive presidential authorization for the first casino?"

"A million."

"And what consideration would you think appropriate for your ongoing support?"

"Thirty percent and we can get licenses made up within a week."

Meyer smiled and sat back in his seat. David looked at Alex, who had let Meyer do all the talking. After all, the man had been schmoozing the *meeskait* since before the Havana conference where Benny Siegel's fate was sealed.

"And what about me?"

All heads turned to stare at Francisco, who had contributed less than David to the meeting; at least the boy had taken copious notes. Meyer cleared his throat.

"Naturally, we will take care of all our partners in the hotel and casino. What do you foresee as your role?"

He was floundering to demand that the brother justify his existence without saying it in so many words. Batista saved them all from the embarrassing situation they'd been drawn into by his craven sibling.

"The mayor is concerned to receive some appreciation for his local efforts here in Havana."

"Fulgencio, I am sure the president will safeguard Francisco's consideration. Besides, as we build more casinos and the number of American tourists increases, I imagine you'll ensure his office is responsible for gathering revenues from parking meters and slot machines."

Alex bit the inside of his cheek to stop himself from laughing, but Meyer seemed deadly serious with his offer. Batista responded by nodding and standing up to shake his hand. The deal was struck and included the pesos from the slots, although Alex knew that Meyer would exclude any machines in his casinos from Francisco's reach.

"HOW DID YOU think the meeting went, David?"

The three men sat in Meyer's suite in the Hotel Nacional to review what had transpired in Batista's office.

"You appear to have got what you wanted as he agreed to your terms, but I'm guessing this isn't over just yet."

"What a very astute son you have there, Alex. I would agree that I got what I asked for, which makes me wonder if I was asking for the right thing."

"To what extent do you trust Batista?"

"Good question, Alex. The man is driven by his ego and his wallet, and not much else that I've noticed over the years I have known him. So any appeal to either of those things usually gets you what you want. He changed the price of his consideration but he had no problem giving up a casino for thirty percent."

"Have you ever paid more for a casino, Meyer?"

"No, if we don't count the Flamingo which had its own set of issues."

Alex's cheeks flushed red as he recalled the night he sent a bullet flying into the head of Benny Siegel, the man who invented modern Las Vegas.

"So why are you bothered? If your plans come good, then you will own a string of hotels and casinos in Havana away from the hold of our Italian friends which will deliver more gelt than any of us can dream of. What difference will a million going into Batista's pocket make in the overall scheme of things?"

"Alex, you may well be right, but so is David. I am concerned he dragged his brother into the discussions. The guy is a cockroach and nothing more, but what was the point of him showing his face?"

Sarah arrived at this moment to catch up on some paperwork, and Meyer invited her to join the discussion.

"Do you think Batista is lining up the brother to take over the casinos once we've built them?"

"You may well be right, Sarah. He wasn't there by accident."

"Is that why you offered him the slots?"

"Nickel and dime stuff, Alex, and he didn't flinch. If anything, his eyes widened as he imagined counting his ill-gotten gains."

"Sounds like nothing is too modest for Francisco Batista to dip his beak into."

"Fashioning him a small bird table might be the best thing to keep him out of our way and it will let the adults get on with their business."

In the distance, the sound of an explosion and the shattering of glass was barely audible, but both Alex and Meyer noticed.

"Students. They are letting off a little steam."

"Meyer, when people throw Molotov cocktails in the street, they are doing more than partying hard. These kids can see what Batista is doing and they are not happy about it."

"Maybe so, Alex. But that doesn't mean we need to be concerned about them. Not everything is certain in life, but anyone who tries to stand between the general and his ability to earn gelt will discover why this general has an army."

7

MEYER SMILED AS he asked for the check in the Lima Hastiada once Alex and Sarah had finished the dregs of the bottle of local red wine. The food was at best average, but they congregated there out of habit rather than love for the place. It sure wasn't Lindy's.

"What are you so happy about, Meyer?"

"Alex, good things come to those who wait."

"Now we're hooked, just tell us your secret. You look like you're fit to bursting and want to share."

"Sarah, as the minister for the entertainment industry in our president's fine government, I have been helping him devise a strategy to encourage American tourists to vacation in Cuba."

"That's why we are all here, Meyer. Have you waited until the end of the meal to tell us what we already know?"

"Patience, Sarah. All in good time."

Meyer glanced around the cantina and leaned into the table, forcing the couple to do likewise.

"He is about to enact hotel law 2074."

"You should have told us earlier, and I would have ordered the finest Californian champagne this place could offer. I mean, if it's the 2074 then we are on the home straight."

"Alex, there is no need for sarcasm to mask your ignorance. If you hadn't interjected, then I could have told you that this gambling rule allows foreigners to have direct holdings in Cuban hotels and casinos."

Alex sat back in his seat, thought for a minute, and let out a slow whistle.

"Finally, he is letting us in to play at the table."

"The investors must have a million to their name otherwise they don't get past the threshold and there is a quarter of a million fee per gaming license."

"So nothing too onerous, Meyer."

"Listen to you, Alex Cohen. You've got to a point in your life where millions of dollars are easy pickings."

Sarah squeezed Alex's arm. She tried not to show physical affection to him in front of Meyer, but she was proud of this moment and her lover's achievements.

"Don't worry. My feet are still planted on the ground. There is always a corner of my heart harboring memories of Broska and another special place for the tenements in the Bowery."

"If you two are finished blowing smoke then, Sarah, please organize a wire transfer in the morning for the government fee. And I'll need a large briefcase for a withdrawal from one of my safety deposit boxes then too."

"By how much will you fill Batista's grift box?"

"Another quarter of a million. The peaked cap might not earn it, but the gelt we'll generate will make it all worthwhile, Alex."

"Politicians are like every one of us—always interested in number one first and the rest of the world second."

"We live together. We love together…"

"But we die alone."

"DID YOU THINK it strange that we walked the money over to Batista?"

Meyer nodded as they sat down at the board table which occupied most of the space in his dining room. Sarah was still wrangling with the bank to organize the gaming fee transfer, and Alex was at a loose end.

"Some matters are best left the old-fashioned way. Cash speaks volumes and is not the least bit traceable."

"With foreign investment possible, how long do you think it will take our friends in Little Italy to pay us a visit?"

"Not long. You know how the syndicate works now that Charlie is no longer in charge. While I might not have fed all the details to the board, close associates understand what's been going on and are ready to make a play."

"Moving large amounts of gelt which Uncle Sam can't see or investigate is an appealing prospect, Meyer."

"We can all see the benefit in that, wouldn't you say, Alex?"

The two men clinked cups and sipped their coffees.

"What are you going to call your first venture?"

"Montmartre, Alex. I've found a prime location with a run-down shack on the current site. It's a hark back to a chi-chi area of Paris."

"No need to tell me, Meyer. I went there while I was fighting the Great War."

"Sometimes I forget, we only met after you came back."

Alex nodded, and a flash of memory of those goddamn trenches ripped across his brain. The bright lights as the shells landed. Deafening tearing metal. Blood pouring out of a solitary hole in the kid's head. They gave him the Purple Heart for shooting a child. Snap and back in Havana.

"I wish I could forget."

"Alex, I meant nothing by it."

"I know that, Meyer. Don't worry, everything is good. The sooner we get the Montmartre up and running, the sooner we can make some real cash in this town."

Meyer nodded and took another swig.

"I am thinking of bringing in David to focus on my interests in this. If he's earning some gelt from me, then he needs a contract to review. Just so's you know, I only want him working on legitimate business. Our syndicate work is out of bounds for him."

"I completely understand, Alex. I won't talk about money laundering in front of him."

"Thank you, Meyer. I just need my boy to stay clean."

"I'VE LOOKED OVER the contracts as you asked, Pop."

"Why are you looking at me so strangely? You can't hold my gaze."

"They need a lot of work before I could recommend you sign them, that's why, and the other party is Meyer, who is no fool."

"What kind of work are we talking about, David?"

"Bolstering your interests almost entirely. Meyer has protected himself well, but at your expense. To deflect liability away from himself but still keep Batista happy, you are the fall guy if anything goes wrong. Mostly, it is your wallet that will hurt, but my professional opinion is that you shouldn't climb into bed with Batista because there may be more than your gelt at stake."

Alex nodded and listened.

"When I read the documents, they seemed reasonable to me."

"Did you see what was typed in front of you or did you rely on your memory of conversations with Meyer where intentions were stated but not papered when they were recorded? I only have what is written and nothing else. And that is what a court would look at too if anything were to go wrong and Batista sued you."

David was right and wrong in equal measure. If matters soured between them, there would be trouble, but the president was unlikely to resort to the law to resolve any difficulties they may have. The man controlled an army and the secret police, he wouldn't wait in line for a date in front of a judge.

Given that the generalissimo would tear up the contract without a second thought, all Alex had was the intentions of both parties as they were written. No more and no less. Meyer was so keen to create his Latin Vegas that he was satisfied to skip any cracks in the sidewalk. David was making sure there was firm ground for him and Sarah to walk along.

"Your advice is well noted, son. We should try to even out some wrinkles but we must be careful not to insist too strongly otherwise Batista might decide to throw his toys out of the playpen."

"I serve at your pleasure."

"No need for that, David. Just see if you can get the more offensive elements watered down. If Batista reneges on the deal, we'll need a plane ticket and not a court date. This contract is only a statement of intent. It's what you do that you are judged by, not your words."

8

ALEX MET SAM Giancana and Santo Trafficante at the airport, one syndicate member to another. Both fellas were based in Florida and the short hop was nothing special, but Alex took care to treat them as honored guests as soon as they arrived on Cuban soil.

"When can we expect to see Meyer?"

"He'll be over as quickly as he can, Santo."

They were ensconced in the Lima Hastiada, Alex's latest favorite lair. Before they reached the cantina, the two Italians had dropped their bags off at their comped rooms at the Hotel Nacional.

"Sam, thanks again for looking after Sarah a couple of years ago."

"Happy to help. Besides, who wants to put their family in danger? Batista's revolution could have turned ugly on the spin of a dime."

"Thank you, anyway. I can't think of the last time the syndicate met in full. It's been a while."

Sam and Santo glanced at each other, and both men smiled.

"Life ain't the same now that Charlie Lucky is back in Sicily. Other fellas are in charge of the Italian outfit nowadays and they have different views about how to conduct business, if you see my meaning."

Alex wasn't sure that he did, but Sam was right. Without Charlie, the Italian mob had become much more insular. Meyer had commented on it just the other week.

"Sometimes, I get the powerful impression that the Italians are holding their own meetings behind our backs. It's as though the syndicate is no longer the place for bosses to come to discuss matters and reach sensible agreements."

"What do you mean, Meyer?"

"I think they might have set up their own commission to settle mafia issues. If you're not Sicilian by birth or by ancestry then you are not welcome."

"Rules me out."

"Tell me about it, Alex."

He had thought little of the comment but if there was a mafia-only commission, then that would explain why the syndicate had almost ground into silence. The other possibility was that he and Meyer had cut themselves off from the day-to-day workings of the syndicate by moving over to Cuba. There may only be a few miles between the island and America, but it is an enormous stretch of water if you let it be.

"You guys over here for a few days? I can show you some sights, if you like."

"I'm here for the week, but Santo is about to move here."

Alex knew better than to ask Santo why he was fleeing the US, as it was unlikely to be because the Florida climate disagreed with him. His mansion was extremely comfortable according to Sarah, and she had spent enough time there to know for sure.

"In that case, the least I can do is to take you fellas out to eat tonight to celebrate."

ALEX NOTICED THE stilted silence between his dinner guests almost before everyone had sat down at the Nacional restaurant table. Neither Sarah nor Meyer appeared to behave any differently and Alex was left to decide for himself whether it was his imagination or if there was an underlying tension between Sam, Santo, and the rest of the group. The slurping sounds of their soup kept him focused at the start of the meal.

"Sam, how is Vegas holding up without me?"

"All good."

"Do you see much of Ezra and Massimo, my lieutenants?"

"Now and again. I don't spend a lot of time in Nevada."

Alex glanced at Sarah, hoping she might weave a conversational line, but she stared at the bowl in front of her. Meyer gave no sign he wanted to help either.

"Well, let them know they are in our thoughts."

"I'll be sure to do that."

Sam's eyes flitted up at Santo's but everybody continued to focus hard on glugging down their minestrone. Alex thought about Sam's intonation—did he detect a note of irritation? These Italians were giving nothing away and one was going to be their neighbor.

Once the dessert had been wolfed down in record time, Alex felt no need to force anyone into being together a moment longer than was necessary and asked for the check before the waiter could offer them a liqueur or cup of coffee.

"Would you gentlemen like to share a brandy up in my suite?"

Meyer's suggestion received nods of agreement, and Sarah sensed this was her opportunity to escape.

"I'm sure you fellas have business to discuss and don't want a woman to get in the way of some of your more robust conversation."

She understood these Sicilians well, and they smiled and shook hands before following Meyer and Alex out of the hotel restaurant, into the elevator and settling into Meyer's living room in his penthouse apartment.

SAM ACCEPTED A Scotch on the rocks, and Santo preferred a twelve-year-old brandy. Meyer poured Alex his usual Scotch and gave himself a vodka tonic; he liked to keep a clear head.

"Alex, thank you for hosting dinner, but next time, your skirt can stay at home."

Alex's cheeks flushed red at the Italian momzer's words—Santo's eyes showed he meant every word he uttered. Meyer opened his mouth and then closed it again, deciding not to engage with the situation and let it pass if Alex didn't take the bait.

"Santo, she is Meyer's executive assistant, but I accept your point and will remember in the future."

"I appreciate your understanding. Now let us get down to business."

Sam pulled out a sheaf of papers he had stuffed in his inside jacket pocket and attempted to flatten them before placing them on the coffee table in front of him.

"There are several matters we'd like to discuss, which should be of mutual benefit."

Alex and Meyer sat forward in their seats, and Giancana outlined how he and Trafficante planned to exploit the Havana entertainment industry for their own ends, and the benefit of other Italian gangs.

"Meyer, we will support your attempts to build casinos, but we do not wish to be direct investors in these properties."

"If we are to make something out of this country…"

"Hear me out, Meyer. We decline to be direct investors because we need to place a series of shell companies between us and the hotels. You might not look over your shoulder at the Feds, but we sure do."

"I know how that feels."

"Alex, I heard how you kept your mouth shut and your conscience clean when you went up the river—respect."

"I did what was right, and Las Vegas was the appreciation I was shown by the syndicate."

"Anyway, our interest in the building reflects our desire to keep a proportion of our assets offshore but still under our watchful eye."

"That's right, Santo. We ain't gonna act like Benny Siegel and use Swiss bank accounts."

The Italians chuckled to themselves and ignored the fact they were joking about Meyer's childhood friend and that Alex had pulled the trigger on the fella. The Jews exchanged glances but gave no other reaction.

"Forgive us, he was one of your men, we understand that, but he was foolish to rely on a woman and a foreign banker when there were places and people closer to home he could have used to hide his stolen money."

"Santo, let's move on to explain our actual reasons for wanting to invest in Meyer's casinos."

"Naturally, no offense intended."

"None taken."

Alex shot another glance at Meyer to judge whether he meant his terse reply. There was a reason he never played poker with his friend.

"The skim from our Vegas casinos alone is sufficiently large for it to have gained the attention of the Internal Revenue Service, as I mentioned earlier. Those vultures are circling overhead, and we are seeking legitimate locations to place our money beyond the reach of the IRS."

Even a mention of those three letters sent a shudder down the spine of every man in the room. They each took a swig from their drinks.

"Meyer, we hope we are your first choice when you look for funding in each of your ventures in this country."

"Sam, the purpose of the syndicate is to ensure we scratch each other's backs."

"It certainly was."

They were silent for a spell as each man reminisced about his time spent in the past twenty years as a member of America's first organized crime board. Alex thought about all the hits he had undertaken for Murder Corporation, the arm of the syndicate created by Charlie Lucky to handle any disagreements between syndicate bosses.

"Is there anything else you want of us, Santo?"

"Once you have got Batista to agree to the creation of the hotels, we can provide the people to build the places. Some of the finest masons in the world have been Italian."

"These accommodations are always possible, we just need to make sure that there is benefit traveling in both directions. So if you want my influence in the allocation of building contracts, please don't be surprised if you are asked to provide the payment for the gaming license and any other financing that is made directly to Batista's personal bank accounts."

A clink of glasses and Meyer agreed to take Giancana and Trafficante's gelt to help build his Vegas in Havana. Where Sam and Santo came, Alex knew the likes of Frank Costello and the other New York bosses would be sure to follow.

9

ALEX SAT AT the bar, while tourists placed bets on the outcome of the spin of a wheel in the Sans Souci gaming room. The Spanish-style restaurant and stage was packed because of the appearance of some local singer he'd never heard of but he wasn't in the outskirts of Havana to take in a show.

He watched and waited to see what would transpire. Meyer had asked him to pay the place a visit because takings were down in the casino room and there was no obvious reason that should be the case. Fifteen minutes with a cocktail in Alex's palm delivered the answer.

When a seat became free, Alex strolled over and perched by the green baize of one of the three poker tables and bought himself some chips. There were four other guys already playing—all Americans. Two hands later and he noticed the remarkable skills of his left-hand neighbor. He wondered if his were the only eyes to see the cards speeding from the bottom of the deck and onto the felt.

Alex wished Massimo and Ezra were with him as he decided whether to focus on the dealer or the player. When the guy folded and cashed in his chips, Alex chose to follow the cardsharp. The dealer would still be standing at the table in an hour's time.

Out of the gaming room and into the main bar, the tourist ordered a mojito and sipped it while perched on a high stool. Alex stood next to him and waited with a beer in his hand.

"Been a good night for you?"

"Can't complain, Mac."

"We were at the poker table together."

"Uh-huh."

"You had some lucky hands."

"No luck about it, Mac."

"Well, we can agree on that. You had more than a little help from the dealer, didn't you?"

For the first time since Alex struck up the conversation, Norman Hawkins turned to face him, menace in his eyes.

"What you talking about?"

"The name's Alex Cohen and I'm saying I saw the dealer pass you cards from the bottom of the deck, so your winnings weren't down to luck at all."

Norman straightened his back and Alex considered whether he was going to take a swing at the one-time leader of Murder Corporation. The spine curved again and Norman relaxed into his drink, with a smirk on his face.

"That's what you reckon, is it?"

"Saw it with my own eyes. I mean, you're not denying it, are you?"

"Talk is cheap, Mac."

"Call me Alex. Tell me I'm wrong about you."

Norman twisted round again to glance at Alex and took another swig from his mojito.

"Say what you like, Alex. I don't have to respond to wild accusations."

"You have two options. Either you admit what you've done or you continue to lie to me. Do the former and I'll let you keep your fingers intact. Carry on pretending that there is nothing to answer for and I'll give you a personal guarantee that you will scream for mercy before I kill you. The choice is yours."

Alex leaned forward and placed a shoe on the footrest of Norman's stool so that the two men were inches apart as he spoke, but it also meant that Norman couldn't make any bid for escape. The man swallowed and sipped his drink, replacing it on the counter.

"Little man, I suggest you take a walk with me into the office so we can continue our conversation in private."

"If I do that, I'll never be seen again."

"We can stay here if you prefer, but that'll only make me more annoyed and you will receive the consequences of my unhappiness. What's your name?"

"Norman Hawkins."

"What have you decided, Norman? You are an American and so am I. We don't go killing our own on foreign soil."

Norman nodded and Alex grabbed his wrist to help him off the stool and pulled him in the direction of the lobby where a door marked *Staff Only* stood straight ahead. Down a corridor and into the manager's office, Alex led Norman to a chair on one side of the desk and he sat in the boss's seat.

"How long have you been coming to this place, Norman?"

"About a week."

"And you've been winning ever since you arrived?"

"Yep."

"How many people are you working with?"

"I don't want to get anyone into trouble."

"Of course not, but please do not lie to me, it offends me and indicates you are not showing me sufficient respect."

Alex let those words hang in the air for Norman to catch and consider. After thirty seconds, Norman opened his mouth and closed it again.

"Well?"

"There's one dealer."

"He approached you or the other way around?"

"First night I came here, we got talking, and I mentioned I was down to my last Jackson. When it was just the two of us at the table, he suggested I help him make some money on the side. So I agreed."

"How much you make?"

"Five hundred. We split my winnings fifty-fifty."

"Very noble. Do you still have the dough?"

"Nope, blew it on the roulette wheel."

Alex snorted. This schnook deserved to be put out of his misery, but he knew that was disproportionate to the offense. Instead, he inhaled deeply.

"Under ordinary circumstances, I'd demand the money back from you, but you do not have it. When are you scheduled to leave Cuba?"

"The day after tomorrow."

"No, you take off in the morning on the first flight out of the country."

Norman looked as though he was about to argue the point, but Alex's steely gaze put paid to that idea.

"Get out of here."

ALEX RETURNED TO the gaming room and stood behind the players facing the dealer, named Joel Sala, judging by the button on his shirt bearing those two words. After ten minutes, Joel was relieved, and he sauntered off for his break. Alex caught up with him after only five paces.

"Come with me, Sala. We need to have a conversation."

"Who the hell are you?"

"I'm with the management, so don't make this any more difficult than it needs to be."

With Sala's elbow cupped in his palm, Alex escorted the croupier into the manager's office and placed him where Norman had sat only a short while before. The dealer swallowed hard and waited for him to begin.

"You know a man called Hawkins?"

"Don't suppose I do."

"Funny, because he knows you as the guy who has been feeding him cards all week. Does that ring a bell?"

"I dunno what you are talking about, mister."

"I'm Alex Cohen and I'll start beating on you if you continue to lie to me. Have you heard of Hawkins?"

"I don't know the name, but there is a tourist I've been helping."

"Is that what you call it? Stealing more like."

"I had some debts of my own and needed to clear them."

"Who else you been pulling the same stunt with before Hawkins breezed into town?"

"Nobody, I swear on the souls of my grandchildren."

"Don't go dragging your family into this. How much you make from this American?"

"Thousand dollars."

"Are you sure?"

"I know how much money I got."

Alex blinked as he realized Hawkins had stiffed him. It didn't change a thing right now, though.

"Listen to me carefully, Joel. You should consider that money the most generous severance pay you will ever receive in your life. Leave the premises and I never want to see you again. Understand?"

"Yessir."

He escorted Sala out of the rear staff entrance. When they were round the corner, Sala turned as if to ask why Alex was still with him. He got his answer when Alex pulled out a shiv from his jacket and plunged it deep in his chest. Two more stabs and the guy slumped to the floor, a red pool gathering around his corpse before Alex cleaned his blade on the man's sleeve and walked back inside.

NORMAN HAWKINS TOOK a taxi straight to the airport as soon as he woke up the following morning, just as he'd promised, but had to wait three hours for the first flight home. He hit the bar to kill some time and was surprised to find Alex waiting for him.

"I wanted to make sure you kept your word, Norman."

"Don't worry, I got your message loud and clear last night. I'm outta here in a short while."

"You certainly are. Let me pay for your drink so you know there are no hard feelings."

Norman shrugged and Alex threw some notes down on the counter which the barman scooped up. The two men sat in silence while they consumed their drinks. Once Hawkins' glass was empty,

Alex suggested they go for a walk. Norman looked around as though judging the safety of the idea.

"This is a public airport, Norman. What could happen to you here? I want to give you a proper send-off. Perhaps I was too abrupt with you last night."

"What are you thinking of?"

"A parting gift. You select something and I will pay for it."

Norman sat still for two seconds, then slapped the bar like he'd reached a conclusion and stood up. Alex showed him the way to the souvenir shop and purchased Hawkins a leather wallet. After he led him away from the main concourse to an exit. Norman scrunched his face but followed Alex dutifully, nonetheless.

On the other side of the door was the airstrip with vehicles moving along prescribed routes around the terminal building. Norman turned to go back inside, but Alex leaned on the exit to prevent that happening.

Ten seconds later and a baggage car zoomed past. Alex grabbed Norman's collar and swung him round into the oncoming path of the automobile. His body bounced off the front and landed on the concrete. The driver screeched the vehicle to a halt and leaped out.

"He's fine. There's nothing to see here. Go on about your business."

Alex's instructions were met by an incredulous stare, but the revolver in his hand convinced the guy to keep on driving. He strode over to Norman, who was groaning but had not moved since hitting the ground.

"Hawkins, I told you not to lie to me, and you failed to mention the correct size of your winnings. That was a big mistake."

Two shots rang out, muffled by the general sounds of airport activity. Norman's chest billowed blood and Alex walked into the terminal for a coffee before he drove back home.

10

IF ANYONE HAD told Alex that he was going to get a visit from his eldest son, Moishe, then he would never have believed them. He had been estranged from David for all of his son's adult life, and the same was true of Moishe, only the boy still bore grudges from before his teenage years. His other sons had been so young when he stopped seeing them that he was no more than a distant memory to them.

When David offered to take out Alex and Sarah for a meal, he was surprised but thought no more of the suggestion than to accept it at face value. The venue was their local cantina, Lima Hastiada, and the fourth empty chair was nothing out of the ordinary. Just as their drinks arrived at the table, so did Moishe, who sat down, nodded at his brother, and riffled through a menu.

"I bet you weren't expecting to see me here today."

Alex dragged his eyebrows down from the top of his head, stared at his prodigal son, glanced at Sarah who appeared equally mystified, looked back at the recent arrival at the table.

"You got me there, Moishe."

Moishe reached out to shake his father's hand and then stood up to give his mother a hug. At this, Alex raised himself to his feet and gave Moishe a manly pat on the back, which was reciprocated, for the first time that Alex could ever remember. He wiped the corner of one eye as they all sat down again.

The waiter returned to find out what Moishe wanted to drink, and he said he'd try whatever the old man was having.

"How are you, Pop?"

"Just fine. All the better for seeing you. What brings you into town?"

THE MEAL COMPRISED the usual average food and excellent casual conversation. Moishe allowed the others to talk at him and refrained from expressing any of his typical views about his father and how Alex treated Sarah and the rest of his family.

Alex was thankful for that small mercy but as happy as he was to see the boy again, he was waiting for the punchline. The guy hadn't uttered a word to him since the day Alex visited New Jersey before he moved to Vegas. And that was at least two lifetimes ago.

He and Sarah invited their boys back home after dessert and both accepted, although David was more reticent than he would have expected. Alex served them all drinks in the living room and settled in next to Sarah, one hand on her knee while she draped her arm on his.

"In the cantina, you didn't answer my question."

"Which was that, Pop?"

Alex felt Sarah stiffen beside him and caught her mutter under her breath, "Don't start."

"I can't remember you saying how long you are going to be out here. We'd be honored to have you as our guest instead of you paying tourist rates in a hotel."

"Pop, I was vague because I'm not too sure."

"A day, a week, a lifetime…?"

At the last word, Alex glanced over to David and winked.

"Before I can answer you, I need to ask for your help, Pop."

Alex's cheeks went white, and he swallowed hard.

"Me?"

"I know. It's surprising for me to hear myself say it too."

"Moishe, what has happened?"

"Mom, I'm not sure you should listen to our conversation."

"I am your mother and work at the heart of your father's business operations. Anything you have to say to him, you can say to me. Besides, he'll tell me the minute you walk out of the door anyway whether he has sworn himself to secrecy or not."

Alex nodded to confirm Sarah's analysis and reminded himself that Moishe hadn't seen them since they got back together.

"You haven't asked for David to leave the room though."

"No, Pop. That's because he was the one who suggested I should come here. He already knows the trouble I'm in."

"Moishe: spill."

His eldest son took a deep breath and explained the mystery of his arrival in Cuba.

"I'VE BEEN HAPPY at the accounting firm where I work from the day I started. They have looked after me well and accommodated me when times have been tough, which has been rare. Not all their clients are on the up-and-up, but I figured they pay their bills just like anyone else."

"You mean their ways of doing business weren't always kosher?"

"Yes, you of all people know how I feel about criminal enterprises. I say this out of respect for you and how you've treated my mother. Everyone sat in this room knows what you do, and I have made my peace with that. You took the hand you were dealt and played it for all you were worth. When I was a kid, I did not know about the sacrifices you both made."

"So some of your clients are not just minimizing their tax position?"

Moishe laughed at the memory of seeing his father's face in the newspaper when he was sent up to Sing Sing for tax fraud.

"No, Pop, but who are we to judge?"

Alex felt his cheeks warm but he said nothing more on the subject.

"You are not alone in having unpleasant customers, isn't that right, David?"

Alex aimed a smirk at his lawyer son long enough to be certain that they had all seen his joke.

"Criminal lawyers defend whoever walks through the door, I get that, but I am in a very different situation."

David raised an eyebrow.

"For the last four years, I have been representing a particular client and working hard to help them maximize profit while still operating within the law. I cannot pretend to have asked the details of their operations and they have never told me. Suffice to say it is a family business of Italian descent—I don't judge."

Alex shook his head in dismay.

"There has been no trouble between us all this time, but in the past month, they have raised questions about whether I share information on their business activities. I have assured them that their file remains confidential, my reputation relies on that, but they don't believe me."

"How do you know that, son?"

"Last week they told me that if I mentioned to anyone about their affairs, then I would end up at the bottom of the Hudson wearing a pair of concrete boots."

"Who said this to you?"

"Donnie Cavallo."

"Give me the details of his family members and I will pay this meeskait a visit."

ALEX FLEW OVER to discuss the matter with Cavallo in Little Italy and went straight from LaGuardia to the area just west of the Bowery —the place he grew up in and made a name for himself. Despite the years, Mulberry Street had hardly changed. Sure, there were fresh signs above the restaurants, but the same Mediterranean faces walked the sidewalks and perched at tables watching the rest of the world pass by.

Moishe had furnished Alex with Cavallo's address, which was at the Canal end of the street. Alex sat and ordered a coffee at a cafe opposite Cavallo's home to check the lay of the land. One-and-a-half cups later and Alex knew the fella had arrived. Everything that Moishe had told him showed he was a big fish in a small pond. He was no boss, just a regular mobster running his own crew. His mistake had been to use an accountant but Alex understood the fella's family was worried about having undeclared income that could not be vouched for. Alex had experienced their difficulties himself.

Two gorillas stood outside the front of the building and Cavallo walked inside, so Alex paid for his drinks and hightailed it round the back and up a fire escape. How did he figure out where Cavallo lived? Simple. He listened for the shouting and headed for that story. Sure enough, he spied on the man as he argued with his wife over who knew what. Five minutes of berating the woman and she left the room and ran out of the apartment.

Cavallo remained still for a second and that was when Alex kicked in the windowpane, causing the fella to turn around in response to the shattering noise in his home. Alex pushed his way in and reached out to grab Cavallo's throat.

The guy flailed his arms and fended Alex off, giving him enough time to run to the sideboard, open a drawer and pull out a gun. Alex was too quick and punched him square on the jaw. Cavallo lost his balance and landed on the floor, banging his forehead on the furniture as he collapsed. Alex stood over him, one foot leaning on his wrist until Cavallo released the pistol.

"Listen to me, Cavallo. I have no intention of killing you, otherwise, you'd be dead already. Instead, I wish to give you a simple message: leave Moishe Cohen alone. Change your accountant and never threaten to harm him again in his life."

"And why should I do that, old man?"

"You have threatened someone who you must leave alone. That is enough."

"What are you talking about?"

"Moishe Cohen. He has sought my guidance and I have promised to sort this matter out."

"You go back under whatever kike rock you crawled out from and let me be."

While he leaned on Cavallo's lower arm, he didn't notice the younger man's other fist had formed until the guy punched him between the legs. Alex crumpled instantly and Cavallo ran out of the apartment and away before Alex could recover to chase after him.

ALTHOUGH HE RANSACKED the place, Alex found nothing he could use as leverage against Cavallo, but a framed photo at the back of a drawer gave him a powerful idea of what to do next.

That afternoon, Alex waited in a different cafe just below Canal until a black-haired girl sashayed into view. He stood up, crossed the street, and tailgated into her apartment block. She turned her head as he followed her in, but Alex smiled and tipped his hat to put her at her ease.

Alivia Bicchieri ignored him as she walked up the two flights of stairs to her apartment and was pleased to have a helping hand to fight her lock open, what with the landlord not being prepared to spring for a new key, the cheapskate. He stepped back to give Alivia the space to walk inside. Alex looked up and down the corridor, saw there were no witnesses, and pushed Alivia square in the back, making her stumble onto the living room floor. Alex slammed the door behind him and grabbed her by the nape of the neck.

"Please no…"

These were the last words Bicchieri uttered before Alex whipped out his gun and blasted three slugs into her body, two in the chest and one between the eyes. He dragged the corpse into the bedroom, careful not to allow any of her blood to land on his clothing.

He pulled open the bathroom cabinet door and removed a couple of items and shoved them in his jacket. Then a quick look through Alivia's handbag and Alex walked out of the building to find himself an anonymous fleapit to spend the night.

After a rough night's sleep, he headed back to Cavallo's, only this time he knocked on the door as politely as he could. When the fella answered, Alex was ready for him.

"I think you left these in Alivia's apartment."

He thrust a whalebone comb and hairbrush into Cavallo's hands, who looked down and blinked. As soon as he recognized what he was holding, his eyes widened and his jaw dropped.

"You'd better come in."

Alex sat down while Cavallo used a nearby dining room chair.

"I believe condolences are in order, Donnie."

The man looked straight through Alex, so much that he wondered if the boy had heard him at all.

"News travels fast, old man."

"Call me Alex. We had some unfinished business from yesterday. First, let me apologize for my abrupt behavior. I misunderstood the caliber of fella I was dealing with. I should have asked for you to sit down with me and discuss Moishe's situation man-to-man."

"Things have got out of hand."

"That they have, Donnie, but I am here now so that we can resolve any outstanding issues."

Cavallo wiped a tear from his eye and went over to the kitchenette to prepare a pot of coffee. "Want some?"

Alex nodded consent and continued. "I would like you to find a different accountant to look after your business interests and those of your family. To ease the transition, I am prepared to make a modest contribution to your costs and I will, of course, pay for your girlfriend's funeral. Such a tragic loss and she was so young."

He glared at Cavallo, who stirred cream into his drink as he listened.

"Did you have to murder her?"

"I never said I did, Donnie. But you must understand that if you threaten my son, you can be damn certain I shall execute some skirt of yours without a moment's hesitation. Imagine what I would do if you attempted any kind of retaliation at this point."

"You don't have to threaten me, Alex. I've asked some fellas about you and I won't cross you again… She was sweet, you know?"

"I'm sure Alivia was the apple of your eye, but you must believe me when I tell you that you'll find somebody else to warm your bed at night. Whatever you do, my children are off limits, especially as they are not even part of my business. Capiche?"

Donnie nodded and Alex finished his coffee before leaving an envelope with cash on the dining room table.

11

ON THE WAY back to his Havana home, Alex took the opportunity of listening to his taxi driver while taking the hop from the airport. Like every cabbie he had ever met, the guy was hacking for a living because there was nothing else for him to do. He spun a story about his choice to work nights to pay for his daughter's upcoming wedding, but Alex wasn't buying it. He listened, anyway.

"Have you heard about the trouble down south?"

"No, I've been out of the country the last few days. What's happened?"

"The news isn't too clear about the details, but there were a couple of attacks in Playa Las Coloradas, one night after the other, that left two soldiers dead and fourteen injured."

"Did they mention who did it?"

"Not on the radio."

"You know anyway?"

"Fidel and Raul Castro are forming a people's army, they say."

"Should I have heard of these guys?"

"You're a tourist, so no."

"I've lived here for a few years."

"No disrespect, but given where I'm driving you to, you ain't gonna have come across the Castro brothers on your travels."

Alex cast his mind back to his arrival in America and the slum tenements his family called home, while they eked a living out of nothing. There wasn't much difference between his background and the Castros. Why would the brothers bear arms against their government whereas Alex had taken a different path and made the streets his own?

"Apart from giving Batista a bloody nose, is there anything to these compadres?"

"They might not be much now, but I heard Fidel speak a month ago, and he knows how to rouse a crowd."

"You think he'll stand in the next elections?"

"You're kidding, right? There won't be any free elections while Batista is in power. That's what Fidel said, at any rate."

"And you believe him?"

"You say you've lived here a while, so you tell me. What has Batista done for the ordinary joe?"

Alex nodded and allowed the conversation to be devoured by silence. His driver was saying what he had thought from the moment he met the generalissimo. Only now it sounded like there might be someone who intended to do something about it.

"WHAT DO YOU make of Fidel and Raul Castro, Meyer?"

"Haven't met them, but, Alex, I'm not that bothered."

"From what I've heard, they've punched Batista in the stomach."

"More a graze of an ankle, according to the man himself."

"You've spoken to him on this?"

"Of course, Alex. I am pumping a lot of money into this country and I need to know my investments are safe. I have faith that Batista knows what to do about the Castros."

"And you believe he'll carry through with his plans?"

"I don't know if you noticed, but he has a ruthless streak."

He paused for thought and realized that Meyer was correct. The guy may not be much more than an ego in a uniform, but he was a predictable jumped-up long streak of lokshen. Meyer stirred his coffee some more, and Alex noticed the corner of Meyer's mouth turn up into a half-smile.

JUNE 1955

12

ALEX COULDN'T REMEMBER seeing Meyer shine up so well. His tux made his pale skin glow in contrast. With Sarah on his arm, he walked into the Montmartre casino on its opening night with a spring in his step. This was the first venue his friend had built from scratch in Cuba and Alex had also put his fair share of blood, sweat, and tears into its creation.

It felt like those early days in Vegas, only without the tension that Benny Siegel created wherever he went. Meyer offered a steady and sure pair of hands while Alex figured that if they could make this joint work, then they would only be limited by their imaginations. Batista might be a schlemiel in a suit, but he was delivering on his end of the bargain.

Alex smiled at the thought that Meyer had been appointed minister for entertainment by the general and was receiving a salary of twenty-five thousand dollars for his troubles; that some of Lansky's bribe money was wending its way back into his own wallet almost made Alex chuckle.

"Share the joke."

"It's best if I don't, Sarah. You probably won't laugh."

She shrugged as they continued to walk the red carpet through the Montmartre entrance. Well-known faces from the big screen crammed the lobby, along with some less recognizable men who had never set foot in California. These were Meyer's business partners and associates—the Italian mob bosses and other senior figures in American organized crime.

The toasts of Hollywood greeted Alex like he was their best friend and he ignored their vacuous pretense while acknowledging to himself that many of them had performed in his Vegas hotels and were showing their appreciation the only way they knew how.

"Darling, so great to see you here. And who is this fabulous woman on your arm?"

Alex introduced Lana Turner to a star-struck and tongue-tied Sarah, then she blinked and the actress carried on down the line and into the casino.

"How many other autographs am I going to miss out on tonight?"

"Beats me, but don't forget that these people with their big grins and coiffed hair are just a bunch of actors who have done me favors over the years."

SARAH CONTINUED TO stick to Alex's arm throughout the night as they bobbed and weaved their way around the guests and their cocktails. Meyer ensured the casino was open all the time his patrons were on the premises and so Alex looked at the Hollywood high rollers throw chips like they were going out of fashion.

As they watched Johnny Stompanato lose his shirt at the roulette wheel, Alex noticed Santo Trafficante on his other side from Sarah. Alex nodded again at the dealer at Johnny's table to allow the guy who used to run with Mickey Cohen more leeway with his losses.

"You're showing much generosity to Stompanato, Alex."

"A friend of Mickey's is a friend of mine and if Johnny doesn't bounce back of his own accord, then I am sure Meyer will be happy to ignore the debt as a favor to Mickey."

"Johnny is no longer one of our friends, Alex. The guy manages actors nowadays, at least the ones he sleeps with."

"Mickey is still a friend of mine and I'll get the money back in other ways. If he sets foot in a Vegas casino, then he'll be standing on my turf. I can afford to wait to recoup my losses—the house always wins, right?"

Santo chuckled briefly, and Sarah sought fresh beverages for the three of them.

"How's business with you, Santo?"

"Can't complain. The move to Cuba has been good. I am making more money than I used to when I was based in Florida, and there is less scrutiny from Uncle Sam. What's not to like?"

"I understand. I'm in the same boat. Ezra and Massimo, my lieutenants, look after my Vegas interests so I see the same revenue stream but this place is all gravy."

"You talking about the Montmartre?"

"It's only just opened."

"That's what I thought, Alex."

"No, I meant Cuba. The potential in this country is immense, you know that for yourself, and Meyer is one smart cookie with the vision to create a Latin American Vegas."

"There's money in those cocktails, for sure."

As Santo spoke, a waitress arrived with a tray for the two men and Sarah returned to sit next to Alex with a pina colada in her hand.

"To success in Havana."

All three clinked their glasses and sipped their chosen beverage. Just before Santo moved off to speak to some fellas on the other side of the room, he leaned into Alex's ear.

"Don't be too generous with Stompanato if you are a friend of Mickey's."

Alex nodded and the next time the dealer looked at him for permission to take the uncovered bet, Alex declined. As Johnny was about to open his mouth to complain, Alex stepped forward and placed a hand on the fella's shoulder.

"I think you need to try a different game. Let's get your glass filled and see if there is something else that interests you."

Stompanato looked up at Alex and recognized him. His eyes shifted left and right until an item caught his eye.

"I want twenty minutes with her."

Alex turned in the general direction of Johnny's line of sight and spotted a waitress.

"No problem. You go to the bar and I'll arrange everything for you, Johnny."

◆ ◆ ◆

LATER, ALEX NOTICED the throng was thinning out, and he glanced at his watch.

"I thought they'd have stayed a little longer."

"Senators always leave early, Alex."

"Sarah, that's not what I meant—people are leaving."

They stood still as the sea of tuxedos and evening dresses flooded past. Within twenty minutes, half the room had emptied, and the couple walked back to the lobby in case everyone had tired of gaming for a bit. They met Meyer with his hands in his pockets, smiling and wishing his guests well as they departed the Montmartre.

"Do you know why the rats are fleeing the ship?"

"Alex, it's showtime."

He looked at Sarah and back to Meyer, then it clicked. There was other entertainment to enjoy around the corner. Trafficante owned two venues within a block of the Nacional; the Tropicana's outdoor floor show was due to start in thirty minutes. And for those who preferred a more intimate feel, there was the Red Room at the Capri, indoors but air-conditioned. The Montmartre was a fabulous casino, but that was all it was, apart from the odd room for private parties.

"As brilliant as this joint is, we've missed a trick, Meyer."

"What do you mean?"

"Remember Benny's dream of the Flamingo?"

"Thanks for dredging that memory back into my consciousness."

Alex stared Meyer cold. He needed no reminding of the dire end of their mutual friend, the man who created Las Vegas.

"The Flamingo was a hotel, casino, restaurant, and theater. All under one roof."

"You want us to bring Shakespeare to Havana?"

"Don't be ridiculous. Let's bring showgirls, crooners, and some comedians to the city—the sort of entertainers who'll attract American tourists and make them want to bring their wives along to spend money with us too."

ALEX AND SARAH walked away from Meyer in the Montmartre and followed the herd into the Tropicana to see what they would compete against. Alex noticed Santo propping up the bar to the left of the stage in the gardens and spotted several fellas sprinkled around the edge of the auditorium, positioned in case any trouble broke out.

Tonight this was quite unlikely, as the place was packed to the rafters with mob members and Hollywood faces. Alex recognized almost everyone from the Montmartre earlier that night.

The show began with a woman singing her lungs out as the band accompanied her big opening number. She wasn't as great as Rebecca, Alex's girlfriend and childhood sweetheart who had made him so happy during their time in Vegas, cut short by her assassination. Those bullets should have peppered his body.

"You might not like to admit it, but this is a fine performance."

Alex agreed with Sarah because he knew she did not want to hear about Rebecca's singing prowess. Was all that ten years ago? He couldn't remember anymore, and he welled up, just for a minute until he felt Sarah's hand squeeze his fingers.

"She might not be with you, but I am and this man wants to take our order."

Alex regained focus and saw the waiter standing there, wanting them to supply the names of two drinks for him to retrieve from the bar.

"Scotch on the rocks and a pina colada."

"I thought you only had local brews, Alex?"

"Sometimes you need a piece of home."

She smiled and kissed him on the lips.

"Sarah, our shows must be more entertaining than this. Whatever Santo Trafficante can afford, we shall buy better."

13

ALEX WASN'T SURE he recognized the woman sat at the other end of the living room; he could count the time since they'd last seen each other in decades, not years. When he'd received her phone call, he didn't know what to make of the request.

Sarah reminded him that the least he could do was to invite her round to their home as she had traveled a thousand miles to see him. When the doorbell rang, Alex leaped to his feet and scurried to the front door. Esther smiled and Alex responded in kind.

"Are you going to let me in, then?"

"Sure, Esther. Allow me to introduce you to Sarah."

"We've met, but I was still in pigtails."

Alex cast his mind back to his teenage life in the Bowery and recalled how Sarah had been the one to encourage him to visit his family when he returned from the Great War. That was the last time he'd seen or heard from them until yesterday when his sister called to tell him that their father was dead and that she had flown over to Havana to speak with him.

Sarah put out some cakes and offered Esther a coffee or something stronger.

"A java would be lovely, thank you."

"When was the funeral?"

"Two weeks ago, Alex. It took me a while to find you."

"How did you even know where to start, Esther?"

"I saw your face in the papers a few years back when they took you to court. And I knew enough neighborhood people to ask the right questions."

"You're still in the Bowery?"

"None of the rest of the family ever moved away, Alex. You were the only one to escape and look how far you've come."

"Did you leave the family home?"

"I live round the corner in my own place, but somebody had to stick around to care for Mama and Papa."

"And now he's gone, Esther."

"The reason I'm here is that I am worried about Mama and we need your help."

Alex sipped his coffee and stared at his sister, so much older than the person he had framed in his memory, but the little girl had grown over the past thirty years. He just hadn't seen it happen, so there was a massive jolt between what had been and who sat before him. She looked middle-aged and Alex wondered to what extent she might think the same of him.

"How can I help?"

"Mama won't leave the tenement."

"Her husband has just died. She should spend a few weeks wallowing in her grief. The woman's ability to generate histrionics is second to none."

"That's not what I mean, Alex. Of course, she takes a stroll around the block every day. It's a great excuse to gossip with everyone she knows. It is not that, we have a problem with the landlord."

Alex's neck stiffened at hearing those words, and he sat upright in his dining chair.

"What does the *schnorrer* want?"

"Jurek Sokolov wants to sell the property and turf Mama out onto the streets. He's been threatening Mama and Papa for the last two months, and I believe that's what did for Papa's heart in the end. Now he has given Mama four weeks to get out, but she is having none of it. She says she won't budge and I'm afraid of what he will do to her. Everyone else has already fled the building. She's holding out because she thinks her real-estate paperwork gives her the right to stay. But Alex, I know that man'll hurt Mama rather than let a contract stand in the way of a good real-estate deal."

"Leave it to me, Esther. You do not need to worry about our mama."

"HOW DO YOU fancy a brief vacation in New York, Massimo?"

"I haven't been there for a couple of years, so sure, why not?"

"I'd like you to go back to our roots and check out the Bowery while you're there."

"You recommend any place in particular?"

"Visit Jurek Sokolov and make him a reasonable offer for some of his real estate. If he doesn't bite, make it a generous one, and if that fails to work then let's hope he doesn't meet a tragic end crossing the street while you're in town."

"Have no fear, Alex. Everything will be resolved before I return to Vegas."

"Once we get better established here, I'd like you and Ezra to come over and help me run our investments. Right now, I trust you two to oversee Vegas for me."

"Any chance of you popping over here for a vacation yourself?"

"Not for a while, but I'd like to. Sometimes I tire of the sunshine and constant warm temperatures, the incessant rum-based cocktails…"

"Enough already, Alex. Why don't we both visit New York if Vegas is too unpleasant for you?"

Alex pondered the proposal for three seconds and realized it sounded like a great idea.

ALEX MET MASSIMO in their hotel. The smell of New York had hit him before he'd stepped off the train. Massimo suggested meeting him at the airport but Alex knew that these forays into Manhattan were best made as anonymously as possible. The last thing he wanted was to be seen with a kingpin of Vegas just as he got off a plane from Cuba.

They spent the evening in Alex's suite in the Waldorf—chosen for nostalgia's sake, as it was Meyer's home for so many years. Massimo couldn't understand why the airport was a no-go, but one of the most famous hotels in the world was acceptable to Alex.

"Two reasons, my friend. First, I am too old to shack up in the fleapits we used to sleep in, and second, the place is so big that anyone could come and go without being seen. The only person you have to take care of is the concierge and you can buy him off for less than a hundred bucks."

Despite the lavish lifestyle enjoyed by the rest of the guests, Alex insisted he and Massimo grabbed some pizzas and eat in his room.

"I don't wish us to have to worry about prying ears, Massimo."

"Understood. Part of me thought you'd like to go to Lindy's and grab a slice of cheesecake."

Alex smiled as memories of Arnold Rothstein flitted through his mind, until he recalled the afternoon when Thomas Dewey strode in on him and Charlie Lucky, leaving a sour taste to their cheesecake and the threat of federal prosecution. But all that was in the past and Alex did his best to live in the present and enjoy Massimo's tales from Nevada.

Once they finished the pizzas, the two men licked their fingers clean of tomato sauce and Alex suggested they get the concierge to fetch two slices of cheesecake.

"Why not buy an entire round? You won't be back in these parts again for a while."

Alex nodded and issued the instructions to the other end of the phone.

"Now, let's talk about tomorrow, Massimo."

"How do you want to handle this Jurek Sokolov?"

MASSIMO HAD WASTED no time since his original call with Alex and found Sokolov's address before he arrived in town. A taxi to the Bowery took twenty minutes, and they dropped themselves off two blocks away from their destination at Grande and Suffolk, two buildings from Mama Cohen's apartment.

There were still a handful of Yiddish signs above some stores but the sights and sounds were so different since the last time Alex had walked down these streets.

"It's been a long while."

"A *gonif* is still a gonif, as you used to say."

"That would have been Waxey Gordon, not me. I have always believed people can change, only they have to do it in the blink of an eye or I take matters into my own hands."

"Alex, remember we said last night that we'd play this nice and softly."

By the time this advice had been issued, the pair had stopped and were staring at the Suffolk Street residence of Jurek Sokolov. He might have kept the tenements around him, but Sokolov had converted all the rooms in his building into one sizeable home. Rat-a-tat-tat and a housekeeper let them in and invited Alex and Massimo to wait in a front room while she found Mr. Sokolov. Two minutes later, a middle-aged man with a long beard appeared and held out his hand, but neither stood up to shake the proffered limb.

"Thank you for taking the time to see us and for allowing us into your home, even though we have business to discuss."

Massimo nodded and allowed his boss to continue. Sokolov sat in the only armchair left in the room and tilted his head to the right.

"I am listening, Mr. Cohen."

"Two doors away is a piece of real estate that is important to me. Not because of the fabric of the building or its location. Not because of the number on the door or the memories it offers me of my childhood spent in the Bowery. Do you know why I care so much, Jurek?"

"I have done some asking around since your silent friend contacted me and I am told your mother lives there. I assume that is the cause of your interest."

"Exactly right. You are astute and sensible, Jurek. And why do you think I have traveled from out of town to talk to you this day about the building in which my mother eats, sleeps, and spends her life?"

Sokolov swallowed hard and lowered his eyes, scanning the wooden floorboards for an answer.

"I am informed that you have been putting my mother under undue pressure to leave the home she has made since the day my family arrived in America. Is that true, Jurek?"

"I wouldn't describe it as undue, but I would be a liar to say I hadn't encouraged her to go."

"And why would she want to do that? I mean, I understand she has been very clear to you she has no desire to go. Is that your understanding too?"

"She certainly seems set in her ways, Mr. Cohen, but progress waits for no man—or woman."

"This progress you talk of, are you concerned about the state of the Bowery or the profit you hope to make on the sale of your real estate?"

Sokolov thought for a minute, his eyes scanning from Massimo to Alex. He passed his tongue over his lips to moisten them before he responded.

"To be honest, it is the gelt. I have been offered a significant sum and all the other tenants have moved out."

"Apart from my mother."

"Yes. I hoped I might… encourage her to go, but she is a stubborn woman."

"You don't have to tell me that, Jurek."

Both men laughed, but Massimo remained straight faced.

"If I found another buyer who merely wanted to maintain the existing building, would you be prepared to sell to such a person?"

"Mr. Cohen, the offer is high. I doubt if you would find such a purchaser, especially given the overall state of the building."

"I do hope you are not going to tell me you failed to maintain the building in order to drive the tenants out."

Sokolov's eyes returned to staring downward, and Alex ground his molars. Massimo opened his mouth as if to begin speaking, but Alex beat him to the draw.

"The buyer I have in mind will pay you fifty percent above whatever offer you have in writing, and the deal can be struck this week. The condition for sale is that my mother stays where she is, you run the building on behalf of the new owner and you maintain the place to the highest standards and to the best of your ability. Are those terms acceptable to you?"

"Run the building for free?"

"Oh no, Jurek. I will pay you the going rate on top of the cost of any labor and materials necessary for the upkeep of the joint."

"You?"

"Why yes, can you think of anyone better to own my mother's building? Besides, if you know who my mother is, then you appreciate my reputation. I will make you one promise beyond the contract we will sign. If any harm befalls my mother while she lives in that building from now until the day she dies then I shall hold you personally responsible."

"With all the consequences that implies." Massimo's sole contribution contained just the right amount of menace to make Sokolov swallow hard again and agree to anything that Alex wanted.

14

ALEX COULD HAVE insisted Massimo handled the Sokolov situation by himself, but then Alex wouldn't have had an excuse to swing by Miami-Dade and break bread with Vito Genovese. The underboss of one of New York's five families was vacationing in Florida while a small local matter blew over back home; a state cop can't arrest you for homicide if you are a thousand miles away. Sometimes the trick was just to beat a hasty retreat for a few months and run your empire from the county in America with almost as many casinos as Vegas. The two men met at a restaurant in the Italian area of Miami Beach.

"Good to see you, Vito. Thanks for taking the time to visit me."

"Alex, we share too many interests to need an excuse to eat a bowl of pasta."

"How is Albert?"

"Anastasia is doing just fine. He's propping up Frank Costello in New York."

The corner of Alex's mouth curled upwards, but he tried not to let his pleasure show on his face. This was the same Albert who'd stolen Alex's heroin supply back in the day and who would have been happy to see him floating down the Hudson.

"Vito, it sounds as though you'd rather someone else was top dog."

"Don't put words in my mouth, Alex. You're not wrong, but Italian infighting has been a way of life ever since the first Mustache Pete set foot in this marvelous country."

"Anastasia has been a thorn in my side too, and I've been around long enough to know that the Italian families have their own Sicilian rules to play by."

"Just so you understand it is nothing personal, always business."

"I tell myself that, but personalities arrive on the scene that make it hard to believe."

Vito raised an eyebrow and paused as he shoveled another spoonful of tagliatelle into his mouth.

"Albert has been, is, and invariably will be a pain in the butt."

"Vito, he exerts a lot of influence within his territory and is a made man. Some fellas know how to behave and others do not."

Vito nodded agreement and the two men continued their entrees until their bowls were wiped clean with bread.

15

WHEN ALEX RETURNED to Havana the next afternoon, Sarah suggested he should visit the Montmartre Club.

"I'm tired. Why are you hustling me out of my home?"

"Trust me, you will thank me later."

One thing the man had learned over the years with Sarah was that he should always attend to her. They might have had their differences in the past, but nowadays Sarah's voice was filled with reason and excellent sense. They ate dinner together and before Alex could settle on the couch with her and listen to the radio, Alex made his excuses and headed out to Meyer's casino. He collected David on the way as he wanted some company, and Sarah was adamant she was staying at home.

The two men wandered around the poker and roulette tables until Alex spotted someone he recognized on the other side of the room. David nudged him in case the point hadn't become obvious to him.

"There's Aunt Esther."

Alex nodded and meandered over to stand five feet behind her and the roulette wheel, so he couldn't be spotted by her unless she twisted all the way round. Her elbows leaned on the edge of the green baize and she stared straight ahead. She only glanced away from the wheel long enough to take a slurp of her cocktail. Alex ground his molars and watched his sister lose a month's salary in a matter of minutes.

She mumbled something to the dealer who raised his eyes to Alex —she'd asked for credit. He shook his head and took two steps nearer to the situation. Even if he hadn't walked forward, Alex would have heard Esther's response because her voice was heightened with an ugly undertow of anger.

"Gimme some more chips. You know who my brother is?"

"Yes he does, Esther, and this gentleman may not provide lines of credit. It is time for you to step away from the table."

Esther eyed her sibling and nephew, then inhaled as if she was about to start an argument. Instead, she hiccupped and shrugged, almost falling off her stool and into Alex's arms.

"Let's go to the bar and get you a drink."

"Now you're talking, Alex, my boy."

"I meant a java, Esther."

"But I don't want a coffee."

ESTHER, ALEX, AND David sat at a table near the back of the bar with three coffees deposited by the waiter who left them alone as soon as the crockery landed on the tablecloth.

"By your bloodshot eyes, I'd say you've been here since I left the country and have been knocking back the liquor for the duration."

"Do you have a point to make?"

"Esther, you've been in town for barely a week and already you're drowning in the neck of a bottle."

"Alex Cohen, you are the last person on this planet to lecture anyone about the evils of booze. From what I've read, you made your first fortune bootlegging."

"What I did back in the day to provide for my family and how you are behaving now are two different things."

"Keep telling yourself that, bud."

Alex sighed. There was no point arguing with a drunk. Esther's head swayed on her shoulders as she attempted to maintain focus on her brother. David sipped his coffee and kept his eyes trained on his cup or the tablecloth.

"I reckon it's time you were leaving, Esther."

"Let me at least finish my coffee before I go back to my hotel."

"Yes, for sure, but that's not what I meant. You should go back home."

"Nah, I'm having too much fun here. You don't know what it was like being tied to Mama's apron strings. It's one thing to do that when you are a kid, but all my adult life too? She needed me, I understand that, but I put my entire existence on hold for Mama and Papa."

Alex wondered how much Esther's words were the mojitos talking. He'd walked out of his parents' home when he was in his teens—to be in Sarah's arms—and Esther could have left just the same if she had wanted. He had surprised himself at being so happy to see his sister. Thoughts of his family rarely permeated to the top of the pile, and as he considered this, he smiled.

"What's got you tickled pink?"

"How good it is to have you around, Esther. But we can't have you penniless and spending your life in a casino, even if it is one where I exert some influence."

Now it was David's turn to smirk.

"If you are going to stay in Havana, then why don't you work for me—some light admin, nothing more—and then you can enjoy yourself one bit at a time?"

"I want to go to bed."

Esther's head slammed onto the table and the two men grabbed her and dragged her out of the Montmartre Club and into a waiting taxi.

"HOW WAS FLORIDA?"

"Sunny, Meyer.

"I thought that might be the case. The weather's been good here too."

Alex stared at Meyer, unsure whether the fella was being serious as they sat in the Lima Hastiada. His friend behaved strangely once in a while and made Alex wonder if their investments were safe in his hands.

"Did you get matters sorted out about your mother?"

"Yes, thank you, Meyer. There'll be no bother over her accommodation from now until the day she dies."

Meyer nodded, and a smile flashed across his face for the briefest of seconds.

"If only everything could be resolved so easily, Alex."

"What are you talking about?"

"Some of our Italian friends are late with their monthly payments."

"Anyone in particular?"

"I'd rather not say at present as you have dealings with these fellas and I don't want you to change how you treat them, at least for now."

"There might be some trouble ahead, Meyer, judging from the way Vito was talking."

"What do you mean?"

"Friction between Vito and Albert Anastasia to begin with."

"This has been brewing ever since Charlie left for Sicily."

"Meyer, it all started the day Albert stole my heroin route and nobody did anything to stop him."

"Don't dredge up the past. What's done is done."

"I know, but that doesn't make it right. Besides, reading between the lines, Vito sounds as though he has his eye on Frank Costello's job."

"Boss of Luciano's old mob?"

"That's what I'm hearing, Meyer."

"All my life I've worked with those Italian fellas and the relationship has been good for me, Alex. From the days when the Big Bankroll found the gelt to finance our efforts during Prohibition through to our adventure in Cuba. We wouldn't have our casinos in Las Vegas if it wasn't for Sicilian money. Same in Atlantic City. You know what I'm on about."

"Sure thing, Meyer, but why mention it today?"

"Because in Havana I thought I'd be able to carve out a little block of something to call my own without the Italians getting involved. These new boys always have to sour everything they get their grubby hands on."

"And you're still relying on their money now."

"It's not the gelt, it's the way they ask for an inch and take a mile. First, can a nephew visit for a few months until the heat dies down in New York? Then he's shipping in heroin without anyone dipping their beak in the trough. Finally, you're asked to give him a controlling interest in a club or restaurant."

"Whatever they ask, you agree otherwise they'll perceive it as a lack of respect."

"Yep. And I don't need the Italian mob to make money anymore. I have Batista and I am a member of the government. Break the law? I pass the laws so I can do whatever I want and still I'm handcuffed to these meshuggener fellas."

16

BATISTA'S OFFICE HADN'T changed at all since the last time Meyer and Alex were sitting together on the other side of his oak desk. This time, Alex noticed their chairs were lower than his; a pathetic attempt at reinforcing his superiority.

"There's a fly I'd like you to swat."

Alex glanced around for the insect in the room but knew to let Meyer handle the conversation.

"Where and who are we talking about?"

"Castro is still roaming my country, causing havoc and discontent wherever he walks. I need you to snuff him out."

Meyer looked at Alex, who turned his head to one side, unsure of what to make of this request for an assassination.

"With the utmost respect, Mr. President, if it was so easy to remove Castro from the scene then better men than ourselves would have done it for you by now, don't you think?"

The dictator glared at Meyer and Alex wondered what his friend was playing at. He agreed to anything the chest of medals asked.

"His devils are everywhere and I want you to stop them."

"I understand he has taken control of some southeastern parts of this island, but I imagine he has plans in place to protect himself from open assassination."

"You are right, Meyer, which is why I need you to deal with this cockroach. Every day he lives, the people trust me less. This must not be allowed to continue."

"Mr. President, Alex and I do not have a vast army to bring to bear on this matter. We have always been careful to surround ourselves with only our small circle of friends from America, in order to protect you from the eyes of the FBI."

Batista continued to stare but Alex thought his expression had softened as Meyer reminded him of the reality of the situation.

"May I make a suggestion, Mr. President?"

"We are listening, Alex."

"Meyer is perceptive to note that he and I have no army to call on, but your soldiers are already in place. Perhaps we could provide some advice and support to your military leaders in the area on how best to deal with this beetle of yours?"

Both Batista and Lansky sat back in their seats to ponder Alex's proposal. After ten seconds of silence, Batista propped himself forward with his elbows leaning on that desk of his.

"Cohen, your idea is good. You can be my military advisors. I'll send word that you'll start with immediate effect tomorrow. Castro won't know what's hit him."

Before either man could utter another word, Batista dismissed them as he picked up the phone to inform his captain to expect guests in the morning.

"WHY THE HELL did you say that, Alex?"

"Because your president thought we were going to send an army we don't have to the other side of the island and strafe every field, village, and town until the Castro brothers were dead. You and I know that would never happen and then you'd be forced to explain how we failed him. And that would have been a conversation where I stayed home that day."

Meyer opened his mouth and decided not to argue.

"Besides, we can offer the best advice in the world and, hand on heart, report back, that is what we did. Batista needs to treat his soldiers better than he does if he wants to get results like Uncle Sam achieves."

Alex's mind took him back to the foxholes of the Great War.

"Alex, I wouldn't say that Korea was a big win for the US."

"What? No, perhaps not, but would you prefer to be fighting against Castro with a gun in your hand or talking to the schmucks who will have to fight Castro?"

"Put like that, I'll be a military advisor for Batista."

"That's what I thought too, Meyer. Now, I can doubtless convince Ezra and Massimo to take a week's vacation down here and they can talk tactics until the sun goes down."

"Alex, you weren't paying attention to Batista carefully enough. He named us both, but he was looking straight at you. That means he wants you to do it and with no substitutes. Call your lieutenants to join you, it'll look a lot more impressive, but the president issued an instruction that you are taking a trip tomorrow and won't be back until the military feel equipped to deal with the insurrectionists."

ALEX MET EZRA and Massimo on the first flight in from the States the following day and the three men drove to the other side of the island, through the Sierra Maestra mountains, and over to the Moncada Barracks military camp located outside Santiago de Cuba.

They were greeted by the sight of a ramshackle force whose distance from the center of power had increased their disinterest in Batista's proclamations and bluster. Instead, they were introduced to Captain Isidro Leocadio Chávez, who supplied each man with a cigar and poured the first shots of rum before they sat down.

"Izzy, have you received orders from Mr. President informing you of our arrival?"

"Yeah, in this morning's dispatches. Good of you to come all this way, Señor Cohen."

"Call me Alex. When Batista makes a pronouncement, what else are we to do?"

"Havana is far from here and we operate on a different wavelength, Alex."

"So it would appear."

Alex looked around at the makeshift camp that had been in place ever since the Castro brothers had blown into town, causing murder and mayhem to the Batista government.

"Don't be fooled by my casual demeanor. I might think this is a fool's errand but I still value my life and that of my family and ensure we send units out every day into the foothills of the Sierra Maestra to root out the rebel scourge."

"Any luck so far, Izzy?"

"None whatsoever. Every few weeks they attack us with mortar fire or booby trap a road with grenades, but we haven't captured or killed a single one of the twenty-sixth of July Movement."

"How big a force are the rebels?"

"Alex, we believe there are around twenty of them."

Ezra snorted at the number.

"I thought there were hundreds of the guys."

"No, Ezra. You don't need an army when you have right on your side, and that's what Fidel Castro believes. He and his brother say Batista is stealing money from the people of this land and want retribution."

Ezra shuffled in his chair.

"Sure thing, Captain Chávez, but it'll take more than twenty outraged men to control this place. You can't run a country when you're hiding in the hills."

"For now they bite at Batista's heels, but one day…"

Alex raised an eyebrow.

"Izzy, do you think they'll win?"

"I couldn't say, but the people are behind them. There's no food where they are hiding, yet they eat. There's no munitions, but they have guns, grenades, and mortars and bullets. The locals assist them at every turn."

"Have you any idea who in the town is giving them help?"

"Massimo, no we don't."

"Then I suggest you send one of your privates undercover and find out who is in contact with the rebels. Once you identify the individuals, you can take them in and torture them until they tell you what you need to know."

Massimo took another shot of his rum. The simplicity of his idea created a well of silence in the room.

"I don't want to appear rude, but do you have any whisky? Rum really isn't my drink."

Chávez grinned and called for his batman to find some ice and a bottle of Scotch for his newfound friend.

THAT NIGHT, AN unmarried soldier, aged only nineteen, was sent into town to keep his ears to the ground and to seek out any locals who were sympathetic to the rebels' cause. Two days later his body was found on the beach with his throat slashed.

"You were right, Izzy. Castro has mighty big cojones and the townsfolk support him. Perhaps you can exploit their loyalty."

"What do you mean, Alex?"

"Take any man in town, just make sure he has a family. And announce you will execute him unless Castro or one of his men surrenders. Then you kill the guy and repeat the exercise every day if no one appears to save the man or you get yourself a member of the rebel army."

"And if nobody shows, then won't that make me an enemy to the townspeople?"

"I don't think you have to worry about that. If the people supported Batista, then they wouldn't be helping to kill your soldier boys."

"As much as I can see the logic of your thinking, I can't attack my people. If the president ever found out, he'd throw me in jail—or worse."

"Having met Batista, I would say he doesn't care too much about what happens to his countrymen, but I understand why you don't want to follow my suggestion. Do you mind if we stick around for a few more days? I haven't seen my friends in a long while and I'd like to take advantage of the opportunity as we are in the same place together."

AUGUST 1955

17

ALEX SAT WITH Meyer in the Lima Hastiada, catching up and enjoying a mug of the local java. Lansky appeared to spend most of his time in government buildings.

"Meyer, it feels like I'm recreating my old gang from Nevada, only in a different country."

"What do you mean?"

"Seeing Ezra and Massimo reminded me of the fun I had looking after Las Vegas for the syndicate."

"Good times."

"And part of the pleasure was having my lieutenants nearby. This may sound soppy, but I miss the fellas."

"Alex, you've worked with those men for how many decades? Of course, you miss them, like I still think about Arnold."

Alex recalled his early days in Lindy's, waiting to have a word with the Big Bankroll. Happy times indeed.

"But, Alex, we live in the here and now. Remember, those times are gone. Our present is in Cuba and Batista is our meal ticket into the future."

"Do you not think that the rebels will come good?"

"Twenty men, you said?"

"Yep. More or less."

"I can't see them bringing an entire country to its knees."

"The people are behind them, Meyer. That counts for a lot."

"They had a revolution in Russia when we were kids and look what happened there. Same in China. Revolutions are for saps. What we are doing is building something that'll last. By the end of the year, we will finish the Riviera. That's not us refurbishing some old Cuban wreck. It's erupting out of the ground and its rooftop bar is so high up, you'll be able to see America."

"Meyer, I admire your optimism."

"This isn't blind faith that you're hearing. I walked into this with my eyes wide open. Batista is a thug, I know that. He rules this country with an iron fist and the citizens get nothing while he and his family line their pockets at every opportunity."

"And this is a sustainable proposition?"

"Alex, the president pays me for my government role. I pick up twenty-five thousand dollars each year to devise ways to generate gaming income for him. If there's a law that gets in our way, he changes it. That is the power we dreamed of having in the States, and here it is in the palm of my hand."

Meyer's eyeballs popped out of their sockets as he spoke. Alex had never heard his friend speak with such passion before.

"You've been warming up Batista for almost twenty years, haven't you?"

"Yes, he vouched for our safety during his first term in office when we held our conference here with Charlie after that scumbag Dewey sent him packing to Sicily."

"Has he ever double-crossed you?"

"No, I trust him as much as I do… Albert Anastasia."

"So not at all, then."

"Not quite. You may be certain that Albert will make money for himself and if your interests are sufficiently aligned, then you can put some gelt in your own wallet at the same time."

"Meyer, do you think Batista'll outlive us?"

"I don't have a crystal ball, Alex, so I have no clue. Besides, I do not plan that far ahead. In three years, we should have set ourselves up in Havana so that we can sit on our haunches and live off the cash flow forever."

"Or until Batista is deposed by the next dictator."

"There's no one waiting in that line, Alex. The closest you could say is his brother, but he doesn't have the brains to remember to wear pants around the house."

They both sniggered at Meyer's insight as David entered the cantina and caught Alex's eye.

"What's so funny? Can I buy you gentlemen a drink?"

"We're good, thanks."

"You still have smiles on your faces. What gives?"

"Nothing much, David. We are planning our future empire in the sun."

"That's nice for you two. Is there a seat for me at the table or am I going back to the US with my tail between my legs?"

"Of course, you'll be by my side."

Alex touched the sleeve of David's linen jacket and squeezed his arm.

"Once we've got the empire running smoothly, there will only be legitimate business enterprises and you are my consigliere in all legal matters."

"Just checking you weren't planning on deporting me."

"All immigrants are welcome at this table, David."

ALEX WAS CALLED into a meeting with Meyer and Francisco Batista. As much as he disliked the president, he despised the brother more because the guy was clinging to the shirttails of his more powerful and corrupt sibling. Alex recalled the first occasion he'd met Francisco and the fact he had been put in charge of Havana parking meters—and was happy about it. Penny ante stuff.

The guy maintained a broad grin on his face almost the whole time—Alex imagined what he looked like when he was told his mother died and there would be the same stupid expression glued to the front of his head.

"We anticipate a little local difficulty which we are hoping you will help us with," explained the fixed grin before him.

"It depends what we are talking about. I'm only one man."

"You undersell yourself, Alex."

He gave Meyer a long, hard stare because his friend knew exactly what Alex thought of Batista Junior.

"Next week I will impose a window tax in Havana, and I need someone to oversee its collection. Meyer tells me you were involved in a similar process in the United States."

Alex's mind flashed back to his teenage years collecting protection money from store owners on behalf of Waxey Gordon at first, and then for himself later on.

"I have a passing acquaintance with the task, Francisco. Forgive me, but what is a window tax?"

"If your home has a window, then you must pay tax on it to me."

"Isn't the revenue from parking meters enough?"

Francisco's grin faltered for a second, and then he laughed.

"Let's just say I am a touch cash poor at the minute and have a new girlfriend to wine and dine."

"And you wouldn't want her to know you can't support your lavish lifestyle?"

"Something like that, Alex. Please remember that you might be Meyer's business partner, but don't be impertinent. I do not appreciate that tone."

"Francisco, sorry if I have caused you any offense. My comments were my attempt to find out the background to the rush to tax the citizens of this fine city. Besides, apart from the pleasure of helping the brother of the president, there has been no discussion as to any fee for rendering this service."

"Apology accepted, my friend, and we are not communists. For the time you assist me in this task, you will receive twenty-five percent of the revenue you generate."

Alex nodded consent, they shook hands, and then he left the other two men to their conversation.

"MEYER, WHAT THE hell were you thinking of? Why did you put me in that position with Francisco Batista?"

The two friends had resumed their usual perch in the shadows of the Lima Hastiada.

"I didn't know it was going to be such a problem. You've made accommodations for Batista before."

"Meyer, I've helped your business partner, the president. Not that piece of longe lokshen. He's a complete waste of space."

Alex's friend stared at him, stony faced.

"Am I going back to him to say you aren't willing to do the work?"

"Meyer, at this point, I honestly do not know. I feel you railroaded me into agreeing a deal with that man, and I had to count my fingers after we shook hands."

Lansky took a mouthful of his coffee and allowed the liquid to slosh around his mouth before responding.

"I should have spoken to you first, but I didn't realize the extent of your dislike for the man. Had I known…"

"What's done is in the past. We live together, we love together…"

"…but we die alone."

"Exactly, Meyer. You and I are good. Perhaps I could supervise without getting my hands too dirty."

"He does only expect you to oversee, that's what he said."

"I imagine he thinks I have this large mob swanning around Havana waiting for me to snap my fingers and intimidate the local population."

"Alex, back in the States…"

"I'm not saying I didn't used to have that set-up, but I left my best men behind in Vegas."

"Perhaps you should invite some friends over?"

Alex thought for a moment and then smiled.

"It would be a great excuse to drag Ezra over here, Meyer."

"And he could bring some company with him too."

18

VITO GENOVESE VISITED Havana and looked up his old friend Meyer and his more recent pal, Alex. The Montmartre Club was the venue of choice for their first meeting.

"I thought you'd stay in America, Vito."

"We all deserve a vacation, Alex. Besides, Meyer and I have some business to attend to this week."

"Would you rather have a private conversation? I won't take offense, Vito."

"Thank you for your kind consideration, but we can relax this evening and talk business during daylight hours."

Meyer passed over a pile of chips to Vito, who nodded and palmed the lot. "Shall we find a poker table?"

"Why don't we go into the VIP room?"

The three sauntered out of the bar with Meyer leading the way and on to a private door to the side of the main casino space, down a short corridor to a dead end with a reception desk and three rooms, one left, one right, and the other straight ahead.

"Any busy at the moment?"

The receptionist shook her head and Meyer smiled, choosing the middle door, explaining it was the biggest of the three.

He pressed a buzzer when the other two had settled into their chairs, and a minute later a waitress showed up to take their drink orders. After they had been delivered, a valet appeared to remove the extra seating that surrounded the green baize table in the center of the windowless room.

The men sat down and played a few hands with little conversation other than an occasional comment about what was visible on the cards.

"Meyer, you are one smart cookie, the way you spotted the potential in Cuba before anybody else."

"Thank you, Vito. I have my moments."

"It was more than that. This place offers tremendous opportunities that we can't achieve in the US. We are out of sight of the Feds to begin with."

"The lack of American jurisdiction means the FBI can only guess at what we might get up to here. But, Vito, almost everything I am involved with is legitimate. I'm a member of the government, after all."

"You have Batista under your thumb?"

"We have an understanding. He doesn't involve himself in my business enterprises too deeply, and I make sure he keeps getting richer. A simple transaction that works well for both of us."

"Like I said, Meyer, you're smart. My interests in the States generate more than enough income for me, although sometimes it is hard for me to spend my money."

"Vito, when we are unsure of the provenance of our gelt, we need to take great care where we spend it."

The corner of Meyer's mouth rose and Vito snorted consent.

"Which brings us to Cuba with its casinos and hotels under your control, Meyer. You have the perfect vehicles to convert uncertain cash into clean money, right?"

"This is not something I bother myself with at the moment, but you are correct, we could use my Cuban entertainment venues for money laundering."

"If I offered you ten percent of the cash flow, would we be able to come to some arrangement?"

Meyer swallowed a mouthful of his cocktail before placing his cards on the table and stared straight at Vito Genovese.

"A dime on the dollar is low for what you are proposing. For a friend, I'd accept a quarter, but no less."

"Twenty-five percent is acceptable, but I would need your assurance that this would be an exclusive relationship."

"Now you are asking me to leave a lot of money on the table. Let me think about it and come back to you before you end your vacation. Shall we carry on with our card game?"

THE FOLLOWING MORNING, Alex and Sarah had breakfast together on their veranda.

"You were home late, Alex."

"I was schmoozing Vito Genovese with Meyer. We let him win at cards."

"Since when do you trust that weasel?"

"When he's offering Meyer a cool ten million a year to launder. That's worth a few hours' poker."

"Won't that place us squarely in the firing line of the FBI?"

Alex put his silverware down and washed his mouth out with a swill of juice.

"They could trace the gelt to the US border, and then it would be a mystery. When Vito repatriates the cash, it'll come in through a different country, so the Feds will have a hard job proving anything, assuming they could see the connection."

"How certain are you that what you're saying is true?"

"Meyer and I have thought it all through."

"He sure has, but I don't want him to hang you out to dry."

"Don't you trust Meyer, Sarah?"

"Of course, though his interests and yours are aligned but not the same. He won't intentionally put you in harm's way, but you'll be the one left holding the baby."

SANTO TRAFFICANTE, MEYER, and Alex tapped their toes to the show taking place in Santo's Sans Souci Cabaret around the corner from the Montmartre. The man, and his father before him, ran Florida, and he had moved over to Cuba two years earlier.

"We don't sit down with each other as much as I would like, Meyer."

"Santo, you're right. There are times we forget we are neighbors."

"It's a two-way street, Meyer, and I appreciate you coming over to visit me this evening."

Alex was intrigued by what Santo might be up to. He'd stolen Meyer's gaming customers with the lure of a show and the sight of a Hollywood star, yet here he was acting like there was just a piece of tarmac between them.

"There sure is money to be made out of American tourists, and there are so many ways to do it."

"Meyer, the more attractions we can put on in this fine country, the greater the numbers will fly over here for a weekend or even longer."

"A rising tide lifts all boats—that's for certain."

"I agree, and it also offers men like us other opportunities too."

"What are you thinking of, Santo?"

"We both know you have ensured there is no oversight of our gaming activities by Batista's government. Congratulations on engineering that situation. I cannot recall anyone who was in Cuba before you, Meyer…"

Alex's friend raised a limp hand to swat away the compliment.

"…and that means you are in a unique position to help those of us who still have the majority of their assets held in the US."

Meyer smiled and nodded while Alex thought about the deal only recently struck with Santo's enemy, Vito Genovese.

"Money laundering is one of the many services I offer those who I am close enough to call my friends."

"Meyer, would you do me the honor of cleaning our casino skim from Vegas and Florida?"

"My fee is a quarter on the dollar and I would not want us to fall out over something as trifling as gelt, so let's not get involved in any unnecessary negotiation. That is my offer. Take it or leave it."

ALEX STARED AT Sarah over breakfast the next morning.

"Enjoying the view?"

"Of course, Sarah, but I didn't mean to stare, I was just thinking."

"And then you pulled the rug from under my feet. You could have pretended to be in awe of my beauty."

Sarah laughed and Alex continued to look blankly until she couldn't joke his rudeness away any longer.

"What's on your mind, Alex?"

"Meyer has struck a deal with both Vito and Santo for money-laundering services in Havana. The good news is that both are being charged the same rate, so there is no favoritism, but the bad news is that he has promised both men that he will not launder anybody else's cash while they work together."

Sarah stopped eating her toast, putting her current slice back on the plate, and she stared into the middle distance like Alex.

"What are the chances of either side finding out?"

"Right now they are vying for power in the Italian mob, so I doubt if they are spending Sunday afternoons together playing pinochle."

"But, Alex, if you have men working the docks who are your eyes and ears then it is only a matter of time before they notice you shipping out crates of cash."

"There is that point, yes. And if you and I can work that out, why hasn't Meyer?"

"No idea, Alex. But Meyer is not a foolish man. He has the angles covered even if you don't know how."

"Meantime, guess who's caught in the middle as Meyer's placed me as the frontman for this escapade. Yeah, I receive a piece of the action, but when they figure out their exclusive terms ain't so unique, who do you think will get it in the neck first, Sarah?"

"We could go back to the States, Alex."

"And do what? We can make our fortune on this grubby little island, but not if we leave now."

"Better alive and poor than a rich corpse."

"If we hang on for another couple of years, we'll never have to work again. I could become entirely legitimate, shed all my illegal investments, and still live the good life."

"Or wind up dead before we have time to spend one red cent."

Sarah stared back into the distance and Alex followed suit. For a second he thought about how beautiful she looked with the sunlight shining from behind her, but then he remembered the vast amount of money he was hoping to make and gazed into the space just beyond her right shoulder.

19

"THERE IS A new opportunity I want to offer you, Alex."

Like Lindy's before, a booth at the back of the Lima Hastiada was the location for the conversation between Alex and Meyer.

"What have you got cooking now?"

"Nothing yet, which is why I want you to be in on it at the start."

"Hit me, Meyer."

"I thought that as you are about to get an additional revenue stream from laundering mob money from New York and Vegas, you should invest in a new casino and hotel complex I'm going to build."

"The gelt hasn't even landed in my account and you've already spent it."

Alex chuckled, but Meyer's expression remained stony-cold. He never joked about gelt.

"If we knock down a couple of houses two blocks away, we can create a space overlooking the seafront with a casino, restaurant, theater, and one-hundred room hotel."

"Won't the residents mind?"

"We'll pay them off or Batista's thugs will ship them out—that doesn't matter. It's the value of the real estate you should focus on."

"And why me? Surely, Vito or Santo are your obvious first ports of call."

"Alex, I've told you before that there is no need to cut the Italians in on every deal that goes down. I think some ventures should just be with my Yiddishe friends."

"How much are we talking about?"

"First, there's the government license and Batista's payment—that's a couple of million. The construction itself will come in at a little under three million. So call it five million plus the running costs for six months but you'll only need to spring for two million up front."

Alex whistled at the amount of money Meyer was asking of him.

"Meyer, the amount I make out of Vegas is only around a million a year and nowadays, most of that seems to go on maintaining our lifestyle over here. Do you believe I've a hidden stash I can just pull out of a wall and hand over to you?"

"Those days are long gone, Alex. And anyway, I expect you misunderstand. I'm giving you the chance to be a frontrunner for the deal. You are welcome to tap anyone you know to come in on the investment, but it is your name that will be on the deeds."

"And, Meyer, you think I can cash flow this out of the money laundering we are about to embark on?"

"I'm doing the laundering and you are taking a percentage from the proceeds to liaise with Vito and Santo."

"Be a buffer between you and the heads of two mob families, you mean?"

"That's what I said, Alex. Think about it. There's no need to rush. I'm giving you the chance to turn five million into ten within a year if you include the kickbacks that running a casino and hotel offer a man in your position."

"Sounds mighty peachy."

"Just remember that every day you don't decide is one less day to produce money. What would you call the joint?"

"The Panama."

"Why's that?"

"I like the cigars."

"WHAT DO YOU think, David?"

"Pop, you take on all the risk and Meyer makes money off your hard work before you even get a sniff of any profit. What's not to like if you're Lansky?"

"We live together, we love together…"

"And the liability is all yours."

Alex sat back in his dining chair as Sarah entered the room and deposited a pot of coffee on the table before sitting down next to him.

"Are you commenting as my legal advisor or as my son?"

"At the moment, I represent your legal affairs to the world and unless you tell me otherwise, this is a legitimate business, albeit one that you would never get to own in the US because of your checkered past."

"The deal itself is on the up-and-up, David."

"I assume that means the sources of funding are not, and I don't want an answer to that, otherwise you won't let me near any of the paperwork once it is generated."

"David, I will look to you to handle the administration of the real estate purchase and the building project initially."

"If you go ahead."

"There may be ancillary activities to which you should not be party but we can worry about those details later."

"Have you decided to proceed, then?"

"There will be no paperwork from Meyer—that's not how he operates. The man has owned nothing for thirty years to my certain knowledge, yet he swims in cash. He and I will have a handshake and nothing more than that."

"For that reason alone, I must advise against getting involved in this project. If you want to spend five million without having a sheet of paper to back it up if things go sour, then you should know not to do it."

"David, if matters get out of hand and there is a disagreement between Meyer and myself over this, then we will not sue each other and legal advice will not be required."

David swallowed hard at the menace in Alex's voice and he glanced over at Sarah, who ensured she kept her eyes on her coffee cup.

"You can call me risk averse if you like, but any disagreement which ends in violence…"

"This is why you only handle certain aspects of my business dealings, David. Sometimes there are things you do not want to know about."

David's eyes darted left and right, then aimed straight at his father.

"Don't do it. If you don't think the risk of being left holding the baby is too great, then consider what proportion of your current wealth Meyer is asking you to put at risk."

Sarah lifted her head.

"What do you mean, David?"

"Meyer wants Pop to pay government fees upfront to the tune of two million US."

"That'd be all our savings."

"Sarah, let's not get ahead of ourselves. I've asked David for advice—I haven't agreed zip with Meyer."

"And when would I have a say in the matter?"

"If it is something I feel seriously about, then we will have a discussion. We are not at that point yet, not by a long way."

"It sounds like we are."

"No, Sarah. If this had happened six months ago, then I would have paid the gaming license fee to Batista as soon as I walked out of the cantina with Meyer."

"What's changed since then, Alex?"

"As you know, Meyer has got me involved with the Italians and I am not comfortable with the situation which is why I hesitate now."

"Wheels within wheels?"

"Exactly, David. Meyer keeps track of all the various deals and accommodations he has made with every person completely in his head. There is no paperwork for sure, but there is little trace of how interconnected any conversation you have with him is to the rest of his empire. I admire this trait in him but the only way to do business with him is to trust him totally and utterly."

"And do you?"

"Sarah, I don't know. For ordinary situations? Of course, but The Panama will put me in the big league or six feet under and you'll be saying *Kaddish*."

"Would you want to be buried back in America?"

"David!"

"Sorry, Mom, but you know I'll be the one who has to organize it when the day finally comes."

"Stop talking as though your father is dead. I will not have that happening in my house... Alex, look at what this deal of yours is doing to us and we don't even know if it is going to happen."

"We live in unusual times, Sarah."

OCTOBER 1957

20

ALEX SAT IN a diner just outside Providence, Rhode Island, at Meyer's request: "Charlie Lucky called from Sicily and would like you to do him a favor and meet with a guy."

They reminisced over the good times the two men had spent with Charlie Luciano over the years before Special Prosecutor Dewey tried to tear their Manhattan world into pieces. Alex realized he hadn't seen Charlie since the day the syndicate agreed the hit on Benny Siegel and a weight grew in the pit of his stomach as he recalled his first few months while in Vegas. The best of times and the worst of times.

For a second, Alex thought he smelled Rebecca's perfume in the diner, and then he snapped out of his reverie. Joe Gallo had appeared from nowhere and sat opposite him in the back booth.

"Thanks for visiting me in my hometown, Alex."

"My pleasure. When our mutual friend inquired if I could take a vacation, how could I not want to pop over here?"

They both smiled and Joe ordered a coffee and a cookie while Alex asked for a piece of cheesecake.

"You can drag the man out of New York…"

Gallo nodded.

"How long has it been since you lived in Manhattan?"

"A lifetime, but we didn't come here to talk about the places I've called home."

The waitress returned to their table to fill up Alex's coffee mug and deliver the rest of the order.

"Joe, what am I doing here, apart from the courtesy call?"

"There is a contract we need completing and Charlie thought you'd be the one to execute it."

"Why me?"

"You are incredibly reliable and a safe pair of hands, if even half the stories about you are true."

"Who's the hit?"

"Your old friend from Murder Corp… Albert Anastasia."

Alex dropped his fork on the plate and remembered to close his mouth. Then he sat back and took a sip of coffee.

"Someone finally woke up to the fact that the fella's a *verstinkener momzer.*"

"Who?"

"Albert's a no-good snake-in-the-grass who deserves everything that's coming to him."

"So can you stay over for a few days until we get this matter sorted?"

"Happily, but there's been no syndicate meeting to approve this."

Joe laughed.

"You are right, there's been no syndicate meeting, but it has been authorized."

"By whom?"

"The commission has given its approval. The Italian bosses keep in touch and smooth out any problems between themselves."

Alex wondered why the Italians felt the need to create what sounded like their own version of the syndicate, but now was not the time for that discussion.

"I'll kill him."

"You and me both, Alex. It's a two-man job."

"No disrespect, Joe, but I work alone."

"Understood, but on this occasion, we must have an Italian witness to the proceedings. This is no sleight on your abilities, it's just the way of the world nowadays."

"When does it need to be done by?"

"The end of the month, so we have a plenty of time to play with. I suggest you hole up in a motel until tomorrow when my driver will take you to New York and we can meet up again in Manhattan."

WHEN ALEX WAS dropped off in the Five Boroughs, he grabbed a cab to the Waldorf Astoria and took a room rather than a suite; he didn't want to appear too ostentatious. Then he awaited Joe who was scheduled to arrive the next day. For old times' sake, Alex walked across town to Lindy's and waited in line with everybody else to get a table.

He asked for a booth near the back, but the maître d' explained that none were available at present and that one of the side tables was as good. A coffee and a thick slice of cheesecake and Alex got the nostalgia out of his system before he sauntered back to the hotel to remain in his room until Joe called him that evening.

"You could have been hosted with a fella I know in Little Italy."

"I don't get out much and besides, I prefer the anonymity of large buildings over the beady eyes of some fella's wife, who'd pick me out of a line-up if her husband needed a fall guy."

"There'll be no patsy for this trip—you have my word."

"Joe, I believe you, but in three years' time when Anastasia's brother comes looking for revenge, can you protect me then?"

"Alex, you are one cautious man."

"We live together, we love together…"

"And we die alone. I get it."

ALEX WOKE EARLY and enjoyed his room-service breakfast: two cheese blintzes, bagel, fruit salad, juice, and coffee. Then he put on the suit the hotel had cleaned overnight and padded downstairs to the lobby. A guy arrived, wearing a charcoal suit and a black fedora, and Alex somehow knew this was his driver.

Without a word, he was deposited on 55th and Seventh Avenue and strolled to the corner of the building, rested the sole of his shoe against the wall, and lit a cigarette. His wait was short-lived as Joe arrived two minutes later; enough time to finish his smoke and not much else.

The streets were as busy as you'd expect them to be on a Friday morning, and the men hustled up one block to reach 56th. Then Joe guided them over toward the Park Sheraton Hotel and nudged Alex as they walked past an olive-skinned guy, hands in his pockets.

"That's Albert's driver," he whispered.

"Where's he off to?"

"The last three days he's spent with a lady friend who suggested they meet up for a quick *drink* while his boss gets his hair cut."

"On the payroll?"

Joe nodded and winked.

"To the barbers?"

Alex buried both hands in his coat pockets and felt the cold metal of the two pistols as his fingers wrapped around the grips. They stood only twenty feet from the barbershop entrance, and still, the crowd was thick. The main hotel lobby was fifty feet to their left, and you'd have thought more people would have headed there than hang out near the slew of stores that supported the hotel guests and also took custom from passersby.

Joe looked up and down the street and stopped, pretending to tie a shoelace. Alex remained vigil until Joe returned to his full height.

"Let's walk past and decide."

Alex nodded, and they both turned their heads to face the window, but all they saw was a man in the barber's chair, his head wrapped in white towels. He could have been anyone.

"Keep going."

When they reached the corner of the building, they stopped and lit a cigarette each.

"That might not be him."

"Joe, his driver has gone for some fun with a skirt, you know he is having his monthly haircut and that is the joint he goes to. Who else do you think it is?"

"Alex, we can't have him escape. If this is not the time then we should wait until later in the day, but if we shoot and miss then the whole deal will be blown. And that can't happen."

"It's him. Follow my lead."

Alex strode down the sidewalk, back to the barbershop, ten feet away. He thrust a hand in his left pocket and pulled out a scarf which he used to cover his face before he pushed open the door. A quick glance along the street to check that Joe's face was covered too. He walked inside and pulled out his revolvers to take aim, but the barber stood between him and the chair.

Alex yanked the guy to one side, and he lost his balance and fell onto the floor. As soon as the barber was out of the way, Alex kicked the swivel chair to make it spin around and as the fella's torso hove into view, Alex let rip with both guns, causing red pools to appear through the white chair cloth. Before he fired a fourth shot, the chair continued to rotate and Anastasia somehow ripped off the protective sheet, aimed his pistol, and fired twice.

The wall mirror shattered because he was looking at Alex's reflection. Joe hit him once in the back of the head and Alex joined in as they both kept plugging slugs into the body until the only movement was a twitching leg.

All this time, the barber quivered on the tiled floor. Alex noticed he faced the ground—he wasn't stupid enough to make any identification possible. A tap of Joe's shoulder and they stowed their firearms back in their coats as they rejoined the crowd on the sidewalk.

Or rather, with all the gunfire nearby, everybody had scattered, leaving an emptiness for the two men to cross before they ran to a waiting car, parked outside the entrance. As it sped away, they removed their scarves.

"I'd lose the guns if I were you."

"Joe, they'll be in fragments across the city before the day is out."

"I would offer to do it for you, but I respect that you'll want to guarantee that the job is done and the pieces will never come back to haunt."

"You know me so well and we only met a couple of days ago."

ANASTASIA'S FUNERAL SERVICE took place at Green-Wood Cemetery in Brooklyn, and Alex made sure he was one of the few people to attend. Even though the meeskait had lived in New Jersey since '47, his local church wouldn't bury him so his family hunted around until they found a diocese that would take the corpse and shove it in the ground.

Alex expressed his condolences to Elsa, Albert's wife, who thanked him for coming all this way to show his respects.

"I was in the neighborhood and we go a long way back—from before the war."

"Then you know how hard he worked to build his empire and protect his family."

"I know exactly what that man did and will never forget while I have breath in my body—you can be sure of that."

21

FOUR DAYS AFTER Alex's return to Havana, Lansky called him and they met an hour later at the Lima Hastiada.

"Why the rush, Meyer?"

"Haven't you heard?"

Alex's expression remained calm, one eye scrunched up as the question piqued his curiosity.

"There's been an attack on Francisco."

"Who?"

"Alex, the guy's the president's brother. One trip to America and you've come back with mush for brains."

"Don't be like that, Meyer. You spend your life with these people. I see them twice a year and you want me to know what's going on inside your head. Give me a break."

"My apologies. There's been a hit on Francisco Batista."

"Has he survived and do we have who squeezed the trigger?"

"Yes, and no."

Alex saw a sadness overtake Meyer's expression and understood that his friend was hurting even though he himself thought nothing of this nepotistic nobody.

"Will he pull through?"

"He's in a coma right now. It wasn't a bullet, but a bomb."

"For your sake, Meyer, I hope it comes good for him. How can I help?"

"We need to find out who did this—and fast."

"Can't Batista's secret police sort this out?"

"There's not much evidence left, just shards of metal. Besides, both brothers have acquired numerous enemies over the years, so if they rounded up the usual suspects, the jails would be full and they'd be no nearer getting the guys responsible."

"You think I stand a better chance?"

"With Ezra over here permanently, you've got a network built up which is not aligned to Batista. You might have more luck if your fellas make some discreet inquiries."

"I'd have thought everyone knows I dip my beak in the same trough as you and Batista."

"Not the ordinary joe in the street. He knows *gornisht*."

As little as Alex cared whether Francisco Batista was alive or dead, he was very much concerned about the health of his family and the safety of his assets. All his eggs were in one Cuban basket and when he woke up the following morning, Alex understood he needed to find the bomber, not for the sake of either Batista, but for his friends and family.

With that thought ringing in his head, he spoke with Ezra and asked his guys to inquire in the cantinas and brothels around Havana; they could widen their search if they found nothing in the city.

"WHAT YOU SEE and what you hear, Ezra?"

"Alex, men never cease to amaze me. They can get as drunk as they like and remain tightlipped but put them in bed with a stranger and a guy'll sing to a *nafka* until it's time to go home to his wife."

"Weak husbands are never to be trusted. Now I see the trips to the brothels were of value. Do you mind sharing what you know?"

"The twenty-sixth of July Movement was behind it. The night before the bombing, two of the rebels spent gelt in one of your cathouses and spilled their guts to a set of twins."

"You believe the story?"

"The nafkas gave up the two guys before there was even a hint of a reward and described them exactly once there was gelt on the table. Also, they know that if we find out they've lied, I'll slit their throats from ear to ear. They are definitely telling the truth."

"Some retribution is in order. I shall check in with Meyer, but do you fancy popping over to the other side of the island with me?"

"Yeah. I've hardly spent any time outside Havana since I arrived here."

"A road trip it is then."

BACK AT THE Moncada Barracks, Alex introduced Ezra to Captain Izzy, and they sank a few beers to keep everyone happy.

"We still don't get visitors very often, Alex, so it is good to see you and your friend."

Alex smiled and clinked his whiskey glass against Izzy's beer can.

"Always great to meet with old pals, as I think we can help each other."

"I thought there might be something when you rang to warn me of your arrival. What gives?"

"We want to bring back two of the rebels for questioning."

Izzy snorted a mouthful of beer out of his nose.

"Good luck with that. We've been on their trail for years and haven't snared one of them. You come down here and announce you're going to take two home for your supper."

Alex's back straightened and Ezra put his drink down on the rickety table in front of him.

"These are responsible for the attempted assassination of Francisco Bautista."

"I am sure they are—doesn't make them any easier to catch though."

"Let's just say that you follow the army code. You have to, otherwise, every soldier would do whatever they want whenever they want, but we don't have any such restrictions on our behavior."

Izzy's grin left his face, and he took a swig of his beer.

"What do you want of me?"

"All we need is for your soldiers to lead us into the foothills where you last know the rebels were camping and we'll take it from there."

"No disrespect, Alex, but do you really believe that two old men such as you are going to escape detection from those rebels? I have never come across any fighters more terrifying than them."

"And no disrespect to you or your men, but Ezra and I grew up in the Bowery and you don't get a tougher neighborhood than that. Show us the route to the rebel encampment and we'll do the rest."

ALEX AND EZRA borrowed some khakis from the barracks' supplies and followed two boys in similar clothing into the woodland half a mile from the camp.

"Another quarter of a mile up to that ridge—that's where the rebels were seen yesterday. We spotted the smoke from their fire, so either they are getting careless…"

"Or they just don't care."

A smile ripped across the boy's face before he and his companion scurried through the trees and away from the 26th of July Movement. Alex nodded at Ezra and they zigzagged over bushes and under branches until they were three hundred feet away from where the boy had pointed. They hunkered down and waited an hour.

As the stars lit up the sky, Alex saw white wisps above the tree line —the rebels had returned to their previous resting place. A nudge and a finger point to Ezra and he got the joke.

The two men inched their way forward, more concerned with remaining silent and not snapping a twig than making quick footage. After another hour they had halved the distance between themselves and what Alex believed was the edge of the camp. There were a bunch of heads sitting still; it must be mealtime.

Thirty long minutes and they were less than one hundred feet from the nearest head. Then Alex froze as he saw two bodies rise and walk towards them. Ezra crouched under a large bush and buried himself into its center while Alex swiveled his head left and right, desperate to find somewhere to hide—he was a sitting duck where he sat.

Ten feet to the west was another dense man-sized bush, so he tried to get inside it before the men got any nearer. No sooner had he buried himself under the leaves than the two rebels slunk past, talking about nothing much that Alex could decipher.

"Do you think Fidel's plan will come good before the end of winter, Ernesto?"

"Don't talk strategy to me when there's man's work to be done."

And without another word, Alex watched as Ernesto relieved himself over the bush containing Ezra while the other guy stood three feet behind him, both hands on a rifle. As the men faced away from him, Alex slowly rose upright and stepped two paces forward, covering the rebel's mouth with his hand. A slicing motion cut open the guy's throat, and he allowed the body to drop to the ground.

The thud made Ernesto swivel his head to see Alex standing in place of his escort. He tried to find his pistol, but Ezra had removed it from the holster on his hip and covered the guy's mouth, pinching his nose between his thumb and first finger.

Alex strode over until he was inches away from Ernesto's face and raised his knife until the point of the blade was by the guy's eyeball. Then there was a crack, and a bullet whizzed past their heads. Ezra slammed Ernesto onto the ground so that he and Alex could make a break for it. Two more bullets flew by their ears but they could tell that these were random shots in the air. It might have taken them over two hours to get there, but after twenty minutes, Ezra and Alex were back at the Moncada Barracks.

22

VITO GENOVESE POPPED back to Cuba to escape some problems in the States; the Feds were seeking to arrest him on narcotics charges and his lawyers needed time to oil the wheels of justice. Meyer was happy to see his business partner again, but Alex was less enthused. He had nothing against the fella but he knew that Genovese's old rival, Frank Costello, was also in town and that could only spell trouble. Meyer was oblivious, as he had no direct business arrangements in play with Costello.

"Let's take Vito out tonight and give him a good time, Alex. We could have dinner with Sarah, then we men could enjoy a show at a club."

Alex wasn't comfortable with the suggestion as he had already arranged to eat with Costello, but there was no shifting Meyer's opinion, so Alex booked an early meal to give himself a chance to break bread with Costello too. He explained his plan to Sarah, who agreed there was nothing but trouble in store that evening.

THE TABLE FOR four was ready at the Montmartre Club by the time Vito and the gang appeared at the joint. They enjoyed a cocktail at the bar and then settled down to read the menus. Even before their pasta dishes had arrived at the table, Alex was getting restive with half an eye on his watch as he slurped down a bowl of spaghetti hoping everyone else had somehow not noticed him eating at double-speed.

As soon as the crockery had been removed by the busboy, Alex said he needed to make a call and when he returned three minutes later, he apologized and explained he had a matter to sort out and hoped to catch up with everybody later in the evening.

A peck on the lips for Sarah and handshakes for the other two and Alex was out of the club faster than the bullets from the gun barrel that had clipped Albert Anastasia earlier that month.

"THIS IS A swell place, Alex."

Frank Costello looked around the Hotel Nacional and couldn't help but notice its luxury. This was the venue that heads of state and other dignitaries stayed in, as well as any Hollywood stars who were performing in town. If you sat in your chair long enough, you were bound to see someone famous. It saved Alex from having to make too big an effort at keeping the guy entertained too.

This was where the syndicate last met and sealed the fate of Benny Siegel—before Charlie was forced to return to Sicily and Alex had been given Vegas to manage on behalf of all the mob bosses. A nostalgic smile appeared on his face, just for a second, and then his expression flitted back under control.

"I'm glad you like the joint, Frank."

"I'm starved. Is there a dish you can recommend on the menu?"

Alex looked down and could think of nothing less he'd like to do than have another dinner.

"The veal is excellent, but you won't go wrong here with anything you choose."

The conversation flowed well enough throughout the meal and as they were finishing up, Frank opened up the discussion to include his fellow countrymen.

"You see many people from Little Italy round this way, Alex?"

"A few. You know how it is, Frank. Cuba is outside of American jurisdiction and Meyer does business with a lot of different people."

Frank nodded and shuffled his silverware around his plate before returning his knife to its original position.

"You heard about the situation in the commission?"

"Frank, I am not Sicilian or even of Italian descent, how am I going to know anything about what happens in your commission?"

"You have ears and people talk, I thought, you know…"

The man wanted to say something but wasn't prepared to express the idea. Alex felt no desire to help dig him out of the hole of his own making—the second dinner was sitting on top of his spaghetti. He must remember that steak and pasta don't go well together.

"So what's happening in the commission, not that it is any of my business?"

"Alex, have you seen Vito Genovese round here of late?"

A blink and he inhaled before answering.

"Not recently. Any reason I should expect him?"

"Nope, I was just wondering."

How Frank refused to make eye contact showed it was more than a passing fancy, but he wouldn't be drawn any further than that.

"Would you have a problem if Vito turned up in Havana?"

"Let's just say I would not be happy with anyone who was wining and dining him—that mutt ain't no good. If I had my way, he'd have been put down years ago."

Alex raised both eyebrows. He could not remember a time before when one Sicilian badmouthed another outside his family. There must be bad blood between those two and Meyer and Sarah were doing the one thing Frank couldn't abide.

"Alex, the concierge told me that the Kitkatt Club is worth a visit —what do you say?"

Frank's hotel had offered excellent advice. While most of the stage shows in Havana were well known for raunchier dance styles than you might find in Vegas, the Kitkatt was renowned even in Cuba. Its dancers wore nothing that would force your imagination to work overtime, and the waitresses were always happy to take you to a private room on the second floor to entertain you in a more personal fashion.

It was perfect—other than one minor detail: that was where Meyer was taking Vito after they ditched Sarah following a show at Santo's Souci nightclub.

"I've got a better idea, Frank. Why don't I make a phone call and invite some girls back to your room? That way, we can enjoy ourselves until the sun comes up and we won't have to bother about bumping shoulders with any sap tourist who's carrying a roll and wants to show off how he's spending it. What do you say?"

"Alex, I don't know. The Kitkatt sounds cool."

"The girls come from there. You'd be getting a Kitkatt act in your own bed and, believe me, no one else can ever claim that has happened to them before."

A twinkle lit up in the corner of Frank's eyes and he rubbed his hands together.

"Then what are we doing here? Let's go."

NOVEMBER 1957

23

"I SPOKE WITH Massimo yesterday afternoon."

"Oh?"

Alex and Meyer were having a quick lunch at the Lima Hastiada; Meyer perused the paper while Alex sat and watched.

"Guess where he's off to tomorrow."

"No idea, Alex."

"That's my point. There's a meeting of the bosses and you have no clue about it."

Alex's friend dropped his newspaper onto the table and ground his molars.

"What are you talking about?"

"You heard. Their banker has not been invited to a get-together of the bosses of America."

"Did Massimo mention who was on the guest list?"

"He wasn't told who would be there. When he got the call, they gave him the location and said to bring only one fella with him. Although he didn't say this to me, reading between the lines, you have to be Italian to have received the golden ticket."

"Alex, Charlie Lucky understood the Jews and Italians succeed more by working together than apart, but this new breed doesn't get the joke."

"I doubt if the ones in charge are that young. Isn't it more likely to be someone like Vito or Frank calling the shots?"

Meyer thought for a moment and nodded. This wasn't the handiwork of some up-and-coming joe. Then he shared his thoughts.

"It would be Genovese, not Costello. When he was over here, Vito told me he was planning a big push to convince the other members of his gang to proclaim him their new leader. Costello has tried his best, but it isn't working out."

"Says the fella who wants to topple him."

They both laughed.

"Meyer, when I had the pleasure of spending time with Frank, he came across as a lightweight, you see? Stand him next to Charlie and you have a cockroach next to a man."

"Nobody stacks up against that Sicilian."

"You know if Frank received an invitation?"

Alex shook his head—the financier was working out the odds. But of what?

THAT NIGHT, MEYER came over for dinner with Alex, Sarah, and David. He remained incensed.

"I've a good mind to gatecrash their party."

Sarah looked up from her chicken and wondered what was going on.

"Meyer, do you think that's a sensible idea? If they don't want you there, you will not do yourself any favors if you turn up unannounced. That's not good business."

"Alex, I know, but the amount of time I have spent with Vito, and the amount of money we've made together, you would think he'd at least acknowledge my existence."

"We are not Italian and should let the matter rest there."

David nodded while he chewed.

"Meyer, my professional advice to you would be to only attend a meeting if they have invited you. No good comes from upsetting people."

"I placed a call to Sicily this afternoon and spoke with Charlie."

Alex stopped eating and stared at Meyer.

"How is he?"

"The fella is well. From what he said, he still has influence over here. I thought he'd focused all his efforts on the Italian end of things."

"Influence?"

"He is installing Vito as the head of his mob. That's the primary purpose of the convention."

"Massimo mentioned it's taking place in Apalachin."

"Alex, that's upstate New York—they held a meeting there last year."

"Did you go to that one?"

"Yes, I was welcome then, when there was money laundering to organize through Cuban hotels."

"You sound bitter."

"Alex, call it resentment for now."

"You'll lose your appetite at this rate."

"Sarah, this is business. My ego is dented, but this is about how I am treated as a partner by these Italian hoods."

"Are you including Charlie in that?"

"Alex, I honestly don't know."

"MASSIMO, I HEARD there was some trouble. What happened?"

"It was an ambush. The Feds arrested dozens of fellas."

"How did you get away?"

"I ran fast—seriously. We arrived at Joe the Barber's house. He'd set up a boardroom in his summerhouse and his men were at the main gate to check everybody in."

"So far, so good."

"Yeah. When I drove through the town, I felt as though there were more local cops on the street than usual, but I thought I was being paranoid."

"And when you were at the meeting?"

"Alex, we were settling down to discuss business—Genovese announced it was time to start the meeting—when one fella shouted and pointed out of the window. There was a horde of cops running through the wood beyond the summerhouse, heading straight for us."

"How did Vito respond?"

"I've got no idea. We stared through the glass for a second or two, and then everybody ran for the door. I was lucky because I was on the third row of chairs on the outer ring—the made men who are members of the inner circle of the commission couldn't push past us."

"And how did you get out of Joe's grounds?"

"My first thought was to rush at the main gate, but as soon as I got out of the summerhouse, I saw that's what was in everyone else's mind. So I took off in the opposite direction to the house and the woods. Over a wall and kept on running. I ditched my gun in a stream at some point, in case I got picked up later. Then a long walk back to town and a taxi to the nearest station."

"You find out what happened to the rest of the fellas, Massimo?"

"The Feds arrested most, from what I heard when I reached Apalachin Main Street."

"Vito?"

"Wouldn't be surprised. I mean, the chiefs were the last out of the summerhouse and the speed of those Feds meant those fellas must have been caught."

"So that means they've arrested every boss in America?"

"Not by a long way. There was nobody from Chicago or California that I could see. It was a select band of a hundred or so, but not everyone."

"MEYER, I HAVE to ask you something."

"Go ahead, Alex. No secrets between friends. We live together, we love together."

"Did you drop a dime to the Feds over the Apalachin meeting?"

Meyer stirred his coffee as the two men sat in his home that night. Their respective families had long gone to bed, and the men were alone. Meyer smiled at Alex and sipped his drink.

"I'm surprised you need to ask me such a question, Alex."

"And I'm noticing you haven't answered me."

"What benefit would I gain by having Vito's nose bent out of shape when he would have taken over his mob and prevented those Italians from splitting up Anastasia's narcotics business operations?"

"You tell me. Costello was out of the top seat, and Vito needed to consolidate his power base. When you spoke with Charlie, did he explain to you what his plans were regarding Genovese?"

"Alex, Charlie Lucky wanted a smooth handover of power from Frank to his successor."

"I'll ask you one more time. Did Charlie want that person to be Vito?"

Another curled lip and nothing more.

"I was fortunate not to get invited in the end, wasn't I, Alex?"

"Sure, Meyer. The price of it all is that Hoover can't pretend there's no such thing as organized crime—not with his men charging fifty or more with attending a mob meeting."

"Alex, whoever chose the same venue as the previous commission meeting is a marked man—what a *schmendrick*."

"You think the syndicate will ever meet again?"

"Not in our lifetime. All that's left is the Italian commission and we are not welcome at the table. Be grateful we are living the high life in Havana. Times in America are only going to get harder, my friend."

24

"HAVE YOU SEEN Esther?"

"Not in the last couple of weeks, David. Why do you ask?"

Alex's son stared at the floor and the kid had trouble written all over his face, mixed with the embarrassment of telling his father that his sister was in desperate need of help.

"She's almost fallen into a tequila bottle and I'm not sure she will ever swim out, Pop."

"Booze?"

A nod from David.

"Anything more than that?"

A shake of David's head and Alex relaxed. There was so much else Esther could have got involved in.

"Where does she prop up a bar?"

"Montmartre Club. It's one reason there's only alcohol coursing through her veins; nobody would try to do anything to a family member of Alex Cohen in the middle of Meyer Lansky's joint."

"Do you think she'll be there now?"

"The place is open, isn't it? Then you can find her with an elbow on the bar and a cocktail in the other hand."

"How long has she been like this?"

"When did she arrive in Havana? About a week after that."

"This is no joking matter, David."

"You're right, Pop."

Alex discerned the edge of disappointment in David's voice, but neither made of it any more than that.

ALEX HIGHTAILED IT over to the Montmartre and discovered Esther just where his son had predicted. As he approached, the barman nodded at him and walked to the other end of his station to allow the two Cohens to talk in private.

"Hey, Esther."

"If it isn't the great Alex Cohen. What a hero of the people you've become."

He couldn't understand all that she said, but she swayed on her stool and Alex knew not to worry too much—the woman was drunk.

"Good to see you too. Can I buy you a coffee?"

"There's no need, Alex, my-dear. Jose has been looking after me all this time."

He looked round to find Esther's benefactor, but there was nobody else there, just the bartender. Alex pointed at him.

"Is that Jose?"

"Sure is." A hiccup erupted from deep within Esther and she seemed quite surprised it had emerged from her body.

"His name's not Jose—he is Hector."

"The barmen here are all Jose to me. Saves me having to focus on what they're called and frees me up to think about what I want to drink next instead."

With that, Esther raised an arm and waved at Hector, who tried to avoid acknowledging her motions, but Alex nodded and he sauntered over.

"Another mojito, if you'd be so kind, Jose."

"Sure thing. For you, sir?"

"Two coffees and no more cocktails for the lady."

Sometimes, being Meyer's business partner had its advantages; Hector needed no other instructions to do Alex's bidding.

"Aw, don't be like that, Alex, my boy."

"I'm not being anything, Esther. I'd like to have a conversation with you, is all."

"Then let's talk and drink."

Alex drew up a stool and sat next to his sister.

"This place isn't any good for you."

"It's a decent bar when you let Jose do his job properly."

"Not the Montmartre, I'm talking about the country."

"If it's good enough for you, then it should be all right for me."

"Esther, I have business interests here and you've been on vacation for longer than either of us can remember."

She swayed some more and sipped the last vestige of liquor out of her cocktail glass, just as Hector arrived with their hot drinks. Esther eyed her mug suspiciously as wisps of steam scurried upward to the ceiling.

"I have nothing to go back for, Alex."

"You have your life to live—the rest of the family to spend time with. Here, the most you can do is tread water."

"Let me work for you then. That'd give me something to do—a reason to live here."

"I have Sarah and David already working for me. Any more household members and we'd have to form a union."

"And the problem with that is…?"

Alex was silent for a spell because he didn't want to be forced to say unkind things to his sister when he knew the truth would hurt.

"There's no room for you, Esther. It's time you went home."

"Then come back with me, Alex."

"No can do. I have investments here to look after. You are the one who must go home."

A drop of liquid departed Esther's eye and meandered around her cheek before dripping onto the knee of her dress. Alex raised a first finger toward her and wiped the moisture off her face.

"Don't worry. I'll take care of you and make sure everything is okay. I owe you that much and it's what I do."

"Not since we were kids, Alex."

"You'd be surprised."

◆ ◆ ◆

THE FOLLOWING WEEK, David took Esther for a last dinner at Alex and Sarah's before she flew off the next day. The mood was somber, and they served no alcohol with the meal.

"You look well, Esther."

"Ever since the Montmartre stopped giving me credit, it's been impossible to get a drink in this town. Nowhere else would serve me."

"These places all clam up. It's almost as if they are run by the same bunch of fellas."

Alex winked at Sarah, who acknowledged the gesture, and David cleared his throat.

"I'm flying over with Esther to spend some time in New York. Just for a little while until she's settled back in. Isn't that right, Auntie?"

"Don't you call me that. You make me sound too old, but yes, it'll be nice to have the company, if only for a few days."

"Good idea, David."

Alex smiled and basked in the glow of having so many members of his family around him, even if it was only for one evening. He was missing Esther before she'd left the country, and he wanted some way of maintaining the connection they'd formed while she buried her head in the neck of a bottle.

"Esther, how would you like to do some work for me in New York?"

"What do you mean, Alex?"

"Well, I still have investments and ventures that need tending in America. I can't think of anyone I would trust more with those confidential matters than my sister. What do you reckon?"

"I am not convinced. I've spent most of my life looking after the family, not doing paperwork."

"You're a smart woman, Esther. I'm sure you'd be able to get the hang of things pretty quickly," chipped in Sarah.

"While he's in Manhattan, David can find some office space to your liking and we can take it from there. He can show you the ropes and only come back when you're comfortable with what you're doing. Would that be all right with you, son?"

"Sure thing, Pop."

"What do you say, sis'?"

"I don't know…"

"We'll get you set up and you could do a trial month. If the work's not to your liking then—no harm, no foul—you just tell me and I will get someone in to take over for you. If not, then we're all in clover."

"I guess I've nothing to lose."

"And in case it's not obvious, I'll pay you top dollar for your efforts. This isn't charity—it's important work I need doing and I trust you to do it for me."

"Then when you're in town, we'd be guaranteed to meet up and talk business."

"That's the spirit, Esther."

25

ALEX RETURNED FROM dropping Esther and David at the airport, which had given him an excuse to wave Esther off with an enormous hug. Sarah was sat in the living room listening to the radio when he walked in and turned it off because she knew Alex was not a fan of the local beats—he had gained a tense relationship with music since the passing of Rebecca, from what Sarah could make out.

"I hope Esther can get things straight now she's left this place, Alex."

"Yes, me too, it was as though she dived inside a tequila bottle and never got out."

"That might have been what it looked like, but you know that wasn't the reason she tried to drown herself."

"Huh?"

Sarah sighed because Alex was so good at reading people apart from those who were nearest to him; then he was incapable of seeing beyond the nose on his face.

"She came over here because she was desperate to rekindle a relationship with you, Alex. Why else would she search you out after all these years?"

"And I spent most of her stay here without even giving her the time of day."

"We both know how happy you were that she'd made the effort, how glad you were when David and then Moishe returned to your world. But it takes more than hosting a meal to forge a relationship with someone you've studiously ignored for your entire adult life."

"You're talking about Esther, right?"

"Yes. I have never doubted you wanted to be close to your sons—no matter what circumstances conspired to prevent you from being there. But when you walked away from that tenement in the Bowery, it was as if it vanished in your mind as soon as you'd turned the corner at the end of the block."

Alex was silent as he rested next to Sarah, his hand holding hers.

"Did I cause her that much pain, Sarah?"

"What do you think?"

"Is that what I'm like to my family. Am I that toxic?"

"That's not quite what I meant, Alex."

"But I took a quiet, unassuming lonely woman and turned her into a drunk within a week of seeing me again. And what of David and the other boys?"

"He's remained sober all the time he has been with us in Havana."

"That's not what I meant, and you knew that. Am I destroying him too?"

"If you remember, when he first came over, he was a shell of a man. And you've brought the sparkle back into his eyes."

"But now he has been witness to all sorts of conversations about matters which an ordinary lawyer should not hear."

"That's a decision you make every time you talk about money laundering with Meyer in front of him. Have you allowed him to be within earshot of some of your other, less savory, discussions?"

Alex thought for a minute and then shook his head.

"Not that I've noticed, but I had stopped worrying about keeping him away from those aspects of my business life. You are right, I should be more circumspect for his sake."

"If you want him to keep his nose clean, then you shouldn't rub it in the dirt."

"David must only touch legitimate contracts and nothing more. I should be more careful in future with what I expose him to. The boy deserves to be kept away from Genovese and fellas like him."

DECEMBER 10, 1957

26

THE NEWEST RESORT in Havana was Meyer's Riviera, which boasted more rooms than any hotel outside Vegas with a sea view for every guest. Meyer moved to the top floor and lived in the presidential suite from the moment the place was built and furnished. He had nothing against the house he'd bought when he arrived in Cuba but saw no reason to live in such a small place when he and his family could roam around a penthouse whose footprint matched that of the entire hotel complex.

During the second week of December, Meyer officially launched the hotel with a star-studded show featuring local dancers but with an American headline act: Ginger Rogers. Tourists flew in just to take advantage of the chance to see this Hollywood icon in the flesh. Meyer knew how to put on a good party.

After she stepped off the stage, Lansky went to her dressing room, along with Alex and Sarah who was a huge fan, and made small talk and gave compliments until the hordes of tourists clamoring for her attention got too much to ignore. Only when Meyer had thanked her for the umpteenth time and shut the door on the way out did he express his real opinion: "That woman might wiggle her ass, but she can't sing a goddam note."

"Oh, Meyer, what do you know? She was brilliant."

Meyer threw a glance at Sarah to show he disagreed, but they both left it at that. No one was looking for an argument—the feeling in the building was joyful, and there was no need to burst that bubble.

ALEX AND SARAH left Meyer on the ground floor to continue to schmooze with his guests—mainly mob bosses and other business associates. Instead, the couple headed for the second-story restaurant to break bread with Moishe, who had traveled over to the island for the occasion. Perhaps he'd gained a love of Ginger from his mother.

"Good to see you, my boy."

"Did you catch the show, Moishe?"

"Of course I did, Mama."

"She sang so beautifully."

"Better not let Meyer hear you talk like that."

Moishe looked askance at his father.

"Not a fan then?"

"Maybe he prefers Fred Astaire," added David and everyone apart from Alex laughed. Alex wasn't sure he could pick the guy out of a line-up. When he went to the movies, he preferred westerns. The amusement died down when he suggested they check their menus before the waiter returned to collect their order.

"Moishe, how long are you in town for?"

"Not sure right now, Pop."

Alex raised an eyebrow but carried on staring at the menu, pretending he was having difficulties deciding what to eat. He and Sarah both knew he would take the steak because that is what he always ate if he had the chance when they were out.

"That's funny because when your aunt visited us, I asked her the same question and got the same evasive answer. Turned out, she wasn't planning on going home."

Moishe put down his menu and a red tinge entered his cheeks.

"You too?"

He nodded slowly. Alex sighed and sipped his Scotch.

"Spill."

"I'm not running away from the States, but I'd like to come to Cuba and work with you."

"Has everyone decided what they want?"

Alex sidestepped responding to Moishe's statement, and he took his cue from being ignored. Sarah glanced at Moishe, who eyed David and his mother before trying to understand what was going on in his father's mind. The conversation twisted and turned, but Alex avoided saying anything to Moishe about his reasons for coming to Havana.

Once they had eaten, Alex handed an envelope to both his boys and wished them well. Each one contained some chips on the house and he led them all to the casino. Once the two men were settled at a roulette wheel, he and Sarah left them to it and headed over to the bar for a nightcap.

"DO YOU WANT Moishe to join the family business?"

"That depends which of the two family businesses you are talking about, doesn't it, Sarah?"

"Would you want him involved on the same basis as David?"

"At most, yes."

"Why the note of caution, Alex? If you are okay with David operating the legitimate side of your affairs, what's wrong with Moishe doing the same?"

Alex thought for a moment. He sounded hypocritical when she said what he believed out loud.

"David came to me because he wanted us to connect again, then we found him work. The only time Moishe has come to me during his adulthood has been to ask for me to save him, and now he wants me to pay him to work. There is the difference, I'd say. Besides, whenever someone says they are not running away, you find that is exactly what they are doing, and lying to me is not the greatest start to a business relationship."

ALEX SAUNTERED BACK to the casino and found that Moishe and David had separated; Moishe had stayed at the wheel of fortune and David had sought the pleasures of a poker table. His father tapped him on the shoulder and indicated he wanted to talk. Moishe looked down at his not inconsiderable winnings, thought for a second, and cashed in his chips, being careful to return Alex's seed capital with ten percent interest.

They walked out of the casino and Alex found a quiet staff room where they could take the coffees Alex had bought along the way and talk in private.

"Pop, I have a wide range of business experience and from what David has told me, it sounds like you could benefit from some sound financial advice."

"Could I?"

"Aw, it's not a criticism. I just mean that he mentioned you were looking to make some significant investments in Cuba, and I thought getting information about tax matters from a trusted source would be useful for you, and I'd love for us to work together. To be honest, I'm resentful of how happy David has been since he moved here. I want some of that."

Alex stirred his coffee. Moishe was right. David and he had got closer since the fella's arrival in town, and the work was the glue that kept them together. After all, Alex was not a natural family man and had spent his life keeping himself to himself and protecting his family from the evils of his work.

"Moishe, to be honest, I am not too sure if that is the best thing for us to do. And before you pull that expression, let me explain my thinking."

His son tried to remove the sulk from his face but looked as though he was having a mild seizure and Alex couldn't help but raise a smile.

"When you last visited me, it was to ask for my help, which you received with a glad heart on my account. We had both been foolish to allow the silence to build between us, and as your father, I allowed that situation to occur. I apologize to you for that. I thought I was doing the right thing by having nothing to do with you boys so that the business I was in would not taint you."

Another sip and Alex wiped his lips on the back of his hand.

"Now, we are both men and you come to me asking to work for me, to be my accountant. And I respect you for doing that. I do not imagine for one moment that it has been easy for you to approach me and ask such a thing when in earlier days, you were so appalled and disgusted by what I do. That takes balls, son."

Moishe allowed a half-smile to flow across his mouth, but he knew he was being prepared for a kiss-off.

"I believe you when you say you are not running away from anything, despite the issues you had with a certain client in the past. But I wonder, why now?"

"There's no particular reason, Pop. I'm in a lull at the moment and having only one client appeals to me. The idea of getting deeply involved in the full details of one business sounds great. Sticking around throughout the year and seeing the complete consequences of everything you do. When you are a jobbing accountant, you mostly prepare end-of-year accounts and tax returns."

"Moishe, I can see how your experience would be useful to me and you are right to play on my old dealings with the internal revenue, but that is not enough. I would be thrilled for us to see more of each other and you are welcome to stay here as long as you want, but I believe you should return to the United States."

"Why do you trust David with your business affairs and not me?"

"That is not the situation. I am happy for you to look after my fiscal affairs… but in America. At the moment, your aunt Esther is settling into our New York offices and I would like you to join her there and manage my US finances."

At the back of his mind, Alex didn't like the idea of all his closest family huddled on this one small island. Despite his faith in Meyer's plans, a part of him wanted to secure a base back home.

27

MOISHE AND ALEX sauntered back to the casino and checked how David was faring. When they'd left, there were only a handful of chips in front of him, but his eggs were sunny-side up on their return. He was smiling as he sat behind a wall of ceramic discs. Despite David's broad grin, his father bent down and whispered in his ear.

"I know you want to stay here but you, me, and Moishe have some business to discuss."

As soon as the words had left Alex's lips, David folded his hand and walked away. The chips could wait until later, and no one was going to steal them from the son of Alex Cohen.

He took the two men to the bar where the maître d' secured a quiet booth at the back, half-lit and away from the other guests—just the way Alex liked it.

"First, David, let me introduce you to our new recruit."

"Mazel tov."

"He will manage my American financial interests from an accounting perspective. Of course, you continue to be my US legal eagle."

David slapped his brother on the back to welcome him to the legitimate Cohen crew. The only other member was Sarah, and she had gone home after the excitement of seeing Ginger Rogers and the concerns about Moishe's safety. Alex reckoned she'd be pleased with the outcome. He'd look after his son without tying him to Cuba like the rest of them.

"Meyer keeps making me an offer he says I shouldn't refuse, but I am not too sure. He thinks I should invest in a new entertainment resort in Havana. It's called The Panama and will be the usual mix of hotel, casino, restaurant, and stage—just like Benny Siegel envisaged for his Las Vegas joints."

David and Moishe glanced at each other as neither wanted to be the first to speak. Alex noticed their reticence and filled in the silence with more details: the upfront size of the investment, the opportunities to achieve profit, and the risks as he saw them.

"As minister for entertainment, Meyer will wave through any paperwork we generate, so that end is fine, but we need to make certain payments to Batista in order to grease the wheels of government."

"Are you saying you have to pay off the president to get a gaming license?"

"I don't call it a bribe because Batista doesn't. He prefers for everyone to think of it as a personal donation paid directly into an overseas bank account. And if you don't make the payment, then you don't get the license, even if you pay the gaming fee in full at the time of the application."

"Well, that is a legitimate business expense as you are making a political contribution, right?"

"You're the accountant, Moishe."

"As your legal counsel, Batista's description doesn't sound like a bribe, especially if at some point we could generate some paperwork to confirm the donation took place."

"David, that won't happen and you know it, but we are missing the bigger picture here. Should I invest in an entertainment complex in Cuba?"

His two sons looked at each other and remained silent until David broke ranks.

"What's the upside, Pop?"

"Casinos make millions a month—that's dollars I'm talking about. Once the place is running at full steam, I'd only need to keep it ticking over for, say, three or four years and I would never have to worry about money again. More to the point, none of us would have to work another day as long as we lived."

Moishe whistled because a new world was opening up to him as the conversation progressed. Alex chose not to mention that most of the profit would be generated by skimming the house take at the casino and earning income from laundering gelt for other business associates.

"If everything is as good as you say and the money will flow like wine out of a bottle, why are you asking our opinion?"

Alex smiled at David's caution.

"I don't know how far I trust Batista."

"With the donation? To keep his part of the bargain?"

"Oh no, all that would be safe. Batista makes money along with the owners of every hotel in Cuba. He would be happy to dip his beak in yet another money-making scheme. You should visit the other side of the island. In Havana, Batista has an iron grip on his people, but that's not the case all around the country. The rebels control entire towns and the outlying regions. If they topple the general, then we'll be left with nothing but the shirts on our backs."

David was the first to respond.

"If you believe the rebels will take over, why are you even contemplating buying into The Panama?"

"That's an excellent question. I guess the reason is that right now the rebels are nowhere near Havana and Batista remains in power. Every day that situation carries on being the case is another one for us to make money. If we build the joint and we hold out for three or five years, then you'll find me in Florida with my feet up by the pool."

"Pop, first, I can't imagine you ever sinking into retirement. Second, from the way you've spoken, the twenty-sixth of July Movement won't take five years to attack this city. My advice would be to stay clear of The Panama."

"I may have only been here a few days, but all the risk you've just described sounds like a thing you should want to avoid. A better plan would be to take your money and build something in Vegas or Atlantic City. They are known quantities without the need to worry about insurrection."

"Moishe, what you are not taking into account is my relationship with Meyer—you too, David. He judges people on how much they are prepared to go into business with him. If you refuse him, then you are diminished in his eyes and I have worked with him since I was a young man—from the days of Prohibition. This is the first time he has ever offered me an investment opportunity of my own. There have been many ways we've made money together, mainly through his seed capital and my hard work. This occasion is different. If I say no to him on this, he might never offer me another similar chance as long as he lives. And the fella knows how to turn gelt into more gelt."

The three men drank their coffees and stared at the center of the table, not making eye contact, to consider all the angles as dispassionately as possible.

"You are my sons and I love you, but you need to say something otherwise you are failing me as advisors."

David chipped in.

"The way I see the situation is that you either keep Meyer happy and risk everything you own or disappoint the man, but remain safe."

"Is losing every cent you possess worth the price of making Lansky feel more positive toward you?"

"Isn't that too simplistic, Moishe?

"Not based on what you've said this evening. If there is more to this, then you should explain it, but I can't see why you'd want to put that much capital at risk. We're talking a seven-figure amount, right?"

"Yes."

"And the money is yours, which you've saved over the years as a financial cushion—what the rest of us would call a pension?"

"That's the sum of it."

"Invest in US blue chips and save yourself the aggravation."

"Spoken like a true accountant, Moishe."

"That is what I am and only a few hours ago, you made me responsible for your American assets. What else did you think I was going to say?"

"David, do you agree with your brother?"

"I see things differently, perhaps because I've seen how you operate in Havana. What Moishe is unaware of is the power you wield and the influence you have with the Italians back home. These men run swathes of America and make up an important source of future revenue for you. The fact the cash might not come from legitimate sources is beside the point in this discussion."

Alex added, "One reason that The Panama is so attractive to me is that the profit it will generate can be entirely legal. We would become like any other wealthy family—like the Rockefellers."

"Only with less foreskin."

They all laughed at Moishe's comment and took a minute to settle down.

"Pop, you asked for our opinions and now you have got them. Moishe advises against The Panama and so do I. There is too much risk and not enough upside for the *tsoris*."

Alex still thought the hassle was worth the effort, but the idea of risking everything—including the lives of Sarah and the boys—was too high for him to commit to the deal just yet.

28

HAVING TOLD HIS kids to go home to bed, Alex walked through the casino one last time in case there was a star to schmooze before hitting the hay. Something about a poker table on the other side of the room made him head over and take a closer look.

As Alex approached the four men holding their cards, one face stood out: Merrick Townsend, who he'd last seen at the launch night of the Flamingo in Vegas. No, that wasn't right—at the Kefauver hearing. A touch of the shoulder made Townsend glance away from his cards, and the frown transformed into a toothy grin as soon as he recognized his assailant.

"I didn't know you were in town, Alex."

"Good to see you, senator. How long are you in Havana?"

"I fly out the day after tomorrow. This was a quick trip to show Meyer some support and then back to the States."

"You still enjoy a game of stud. Do you fancy playing a few hands in more private surroundings?"

"Now?"

"Unless you have something better to do. I reckon we can rustle up three or four other interested parties."

Merrick threw in his hand and walked off with Alex, only to be stopped twenty seconds later by a busboy who had collected his chips from the table.

WITHIN FIFTEEN MINUTES, Alex, Merrick, Sammy Davis Jr., and Peter Lawford sat in a room on the first floor with a pack of cards on a table sporting a green baize surface. Many of the big-name stars had already gone to bed, but Sammy and his friend had been hanging at the bar, keeping the crowd entertained with their impromptu Vegas schtick in Cuba.

The group had only played two hands before Merrick opened up the conversation beyond commenting on which cards were face up for all to see.

"Alex, some of our Italian friends are making a name for themselves back in Newark."

"That so, Merrick? I thought you were responsible for the good people of Massachusetts."

"I was, but I ceded my seat to Jack Kennedy and now I represent New Jersey."

The singers stared at their cards and tried not to show their disinterest in Merrick's chatter.

"Yeah, over the last year, the chief of police has noticed a marked increase in criminal activity in certain parts of the city, shall we say?"

"Any particular names come up?"

"New Yorkers who have never seemed to be interested in my state but who are stretching their wings."

Merrick glanced at Sammy and Peter, and Alex could see he wasn't comfortable being too explicit in front of these men who he counted as strangers. In contrast, Alex had known them both since the Flamingo launched and Benny attracted Californian celebrities to perform on stage for him.

"And are these friends causing you any issues?"

Another glance at the singers by Merrick.

"Let's just say they have a different way of doing business than we are used to, and that caused some feathers to be ruffled which I did not appreciate."

"Would you like me to intercede on your behalf over these difficulties or have they been resolved?"

"Thank you for the kind offer, Alex, but at present everything and everyone has calmed down. Last month was a different story."

Alex raised an eyebrow.

"Some mom-and-pop stores were refusing to recognize the right of our New York friends to provide insurance services direct to the door, and sufficient unpleasantness ensued that the local police asked my office to get involved."

"You called out the state troops over some fellas running a protection racket?"

Now it was Merrick's turn to move his eyebrows upwards.

"To be blunt, Alex, I can live with a few guineas coming into New Jersey and shaking down a general store or two. When that causes blood to run on the streets, that's where I draw the line. There was open gang warfare, and every day there was some mobster or other gunned down on the sidewalk. It got to a point where ordinary folk were too scared to step outside after dark."

"And you can't lose an entire neighborhood of voters, Merrick."

"You understand how American politics works."

"I do my best." A smirk appeared on Alex's face as he recalled his first year in the US when he walked bags of greenbacks over to Tammany Hall for Waxey Gordon.

"Did our Italian friends tread on anybody else's toes when they shipped into Newark?"

"You know they did, Alex. What made matters worse was that the FBI has a watching brief over organized crime—ever since the Apalachin arrests. I couldn't ignore the situation. Not only would I be seen to be soft on crime by my voters, but Hoover might have suspected I had a closer relationship to the gangsters than was real."

"Well, unless they've paid you off in the last week or so, it sounds as if you have no business transacted with these newcomers; pardon the observation."

"For sure, we came to an accommodation, but that's not the point. The last thing I want is for Hoover to figure that out. If he does, I'll be ruined."

"And that would never do, Merrick."

Sammy laid his cards down to reveal a royal flush and everyone else whistled out of respect. Alex had seen it build up for a while, or so he thought, but Merrick had been too engrossed in the conversation to pay sufficient attention to his own hand.

"If you guys are going to carry on talking shop, Peter and I might as well go back to the tables outside."

"No need for that, Sammy. Merrick and I can wait until later before discussing more business—isn't that right?"

"Oh yes. No offense to you, gentlemen, but I had to get that off my chest. The intention wasn't to put a crimp in your evening."

"None taken, Merrick."

AN HOUR LATER and Merrick was up a few hundred and the two singers were doing much better than that. Only Alex was down, but he had decided not to win a penny even before the deck was first shuffled. He had hosted the game to make them happy and not to take the shirts off their backs. Alex glanced at his watch, saw how late it was, and stifled a yawn. Merrick checked the time for himself.

"Well, gentlemen. There comes a point in every evening when a gentleman should stop playing cards and seek other pursuits, wouldn't you say, Alex?"

"I'll see what I can organize, Merrick."

A brief call to the reception and five minutes later, a knock at the door interrupted the men's conversation. Six girls in various states of undress stood before the card sharps and introduced themselves to the group. Then everybody moved over to more comfortable surroundings on the other side of the room, where large armchairs and couches gave each man the opportunity to be joined by more than one woman whose aim was to see to their physical pleasures. Alex made sure he was on the edge. Besides, the girls knew better than to inveigle their way into his arms. He was the host, not a participant.

Once shirt buttons were undone, Alex wished everyone well and went home to lie next to Sarah, who needed no fishnet stockings and corset to warm the depths of his heart, although as he slipped under the sheets, she let out one of the loudest snores Cuba had ever heard.

MARCH 1958

29

ALEX PUT SENATOR Merrick Townsend out of his mind over the following months, and he doubted whether the man gave him a second thought either. Although the fact didn't affect him in the slightest, the first night of the impending Passover was set to take place on Good Friday. A week before, the phone rang with Ezra's voice at the other end.

"Sorry to bother you in the evening, but there's something that needs your attention."

"Where are you and what's the problem?"

"Alex, I'm at the Riviera and you just need to come over so we can discuss the situation in person."

Alex recognized that insistent tone and would have been a fool to ignore it. He apologized to Sarah for running out on her dinner and headed over to the complex, where the hotel dick met him in the lobby and took him up to the seventh floor. Still no sign of Ezra.

In room 705 were two men and a woman. Merrick sat at a dressing table in the master bedroom, and Ezra stood five feet from him. Lying prone on the ground was a nude girl. Dead. From Alex's first glance, she looked as though she might have bled out. Merrick's lap was covered by a corner of the sheet and a pile of clothes on the floor showed that he too was as naked as the day he was born. When Ezra noticed Alex's presence, he stepped away from the senator to have a quiet word with Alex in the living room of the suite.

"Have we worked out what happened, Ezra?"

"Townsend rang reception half an hour ago and asked to speak with you. Instead, they put me on as I was in the building and he told me he needed help of a personal nature. When he let me in, I found Lupita Alfaro as you see her now."

"She is one of the regular nafkas?"

"Yep."

"I assume she didn't bleed to death due to natural causes?"

"No. He says he can't remember what he did."

"Ezra, of course, you were right to call me. I'm going to need you to manage the clean-up and see that everyone leaves the building. Before we get to that, let me speak with Townsend."

They returned to the bedroom and Alex bent down next to Lupita. He eased her long black hair out of the way to see her face and neck better. Her throat was red, turning to purple with recent bruising. You didn't need to be a coroner to spot the holes in her chest and the scissors lying between her and the bed. Alex counted at least three bottles of tequila strewn empty on the floor. He stood back up and turned to the senator.

"How's Sylvia?"

"Huh?"

"Your wife, Merrick. How are Sylvia and the kids? I haven't seen you since the launch night of this place."

He gestured all around him to show that he was talking about the Riviera Hotel.

"Oh, they're fine... What am I going to tell them?"

"Merrick, from what I can see, you aren't going to say a word. This girl will not be missed and her body is unlikely ever to be found. We will make sure of that."

"Can you? I mean, would you do that for me?"

"We are friends, Merrick, and that's what pals do. We look after each other in time of need."

"Alex, we were just horsing around. The next thing I remember I woke up on the bed and there she was on the floor—just as she is now..."

Townsend's eyes stared at the smooth skin of Lupita Alfaro and he cried.

"She was always such a gentle child."

"You'd met her before?"

"Whenever I'd had the good fortune to visit the Riviera, I'd ask for her. To assist me through the loneliness of the nights."

"I understand, Merrick."

"I recall us drinking and joking and getting intimate, and then I must have blacked out. When I woke up, there she was."

"So you said."

"I tried to revive her, but she was already cold to the touch. I didn't know what I was doing."

"Of course not, but we are here to look after you now."

Townsend looked up in between his sobs and mouthed his thanks. Alex indicated to Ezra that they needed to go back to the living room.

"Any idea what that butcher did to the girl?"

"The scissors came from a desk drawer, but why he did it? Your guess is as good as mine. I don't buy that he blacked out though."

"He's very careful to not get too intoxicated. Most of his waking days are spent worrying about what the voters in New Jersey think of him, so he is discreet in his partying. But there sure was a lot of booze drunk next door last night."

"What would you like me to do, Alex?"

"Once we get Merrick out of the way, organize the removal of the body. Bury it somewhere outside of Havana where it will never be found. Is there any evidence connecting Townsend to the girl?"

"The concierge procured her after a call from the good senator and the reception staff know he had an issue that needed your attention. Other than that, we're good."

"Fine. Get a camera from downstairs and take a quick photo of Merrick and the corpse in that room. He needs to see it happen."

"Once I realized the situation, I phoned up for one."

Ezra pointed at a coffee table and Alex smiled.

"Well done. Did he hire this place for the night or was he staying here?"

"He is registered here for another two nights."

"Not anymore. Get him moved to a penthouse suite and change the records accordingly. Get some hush money to anyone who came into contact with this mess. Enough so they won't talk and if you think they can't be trusted to keep their mouths shut, bury them in the same grave as the nafka."

Ezra nodded to show he understood his instructions and without waiting for further conversation, rushed back to take a photo before Townsend moved from his spot. Alex followed him to the bedroom and bent down in front of the senator so their eyes were at the same level.

"Merrick, listen to me. None of this transpired. In a few minutes, we'll bring you to a fresh room, which I will comp. If I had known you were in town, I would have comped your entire stay, but that doesn't matter right now. Once you go to your room, we shall deal with the girl and you will forget this ever happened. At the end of your vacation here, you'll return to your wife and children and nothing will have changed."

"Her name was Lupita, and she was the most gentle person in the world."

"That she was, Merrick. But she is dead and you are alive and we need to think about the living. You, Sylvia, and the kids."

Townsend sobbed again, but Alex's patience was running thin. True, the guy was sitting three feet away from a dead prostitute whom he must have killed in a murderous, drunken frenzy. But Alex wanted to get back home before Sarah threw what remained of his dinner in the trash. Once the man had recovered enough to speak, he asked a simple question.

"Why did you take a photo? There was a flash, and I glanced up to see Ezra with a camera in his hand."

"You are confused. That never happened, and I've been in this room all the time."

Merrick nodded acceptance and looked around for his underwear. When he stood up, the corner of the sheet fell away to reveal he was only wearing his socks.

"Let's find Merrick some fresh things to wear."

Alex rummaged through the chest of drawers in the bedroom and found some shorts for the man to put on, while Ezra fumbled in a wardrobe to fetch some slacks and a shirt. That would be enough to take him to the suite. Once the guy had left the hotel room, Alex asked Ezra to get the film processed by a reliable fella and for the negatives and a print to be sent straight over when they were ready.

"Politicians think they can do anything. One day, that photo of Merrick's schlong and that nafka's body sliced to ribbons will be worth a million dollars. Until then, I'll keep it safe."

By the morning, the room was clean enough to receive its next guest and by the afternoon, Lupita Alfaro was buried in seven feet of soil in some woods fifty miles from Havana.

30

ALEX MET UP with Meyer after Passover; his friend took religious festivals far more seriously than he did and Alex wasn't in the mood for a rabbinical argument about a pile of *matzo* and other unleavened foodstuffs. Although he hadn't seen the fella for almost a month, they picked up their conversation as though they had last spoken the day before.

"Have you given any more thought to The Panama, Alex?"

"Yes, but I remain unsure whether now is the right time for that scale of investment."

"If you are cash poor, I've told you I am happy to advance you the money at more than reasonable terms. This is a great opportunity and I don't want you to miss out."

"Meyer, I know it but I need more time."

"That's the one commodity we have so little of. If I was half my age, then I'd be able to get so much more done with my life."

"It's not over just yet, Meyer." A smile appeared on both their faces.

"If you won't invest in The Panama, then perhaps you'll dip your beak in a less risky venture, although you can bet your shirt on this coming good."

"What's this other deal you're hustling?"

"Don't be like that, Alex. I need to do something about the Nacional."

"But you do not own it, or at least I didn't think you did."

"Yes, Batista's name is on the deeds, ever since his return to the island before he seized power. However, I view it as my hotel and I am tired of watching customers come in to eat at the restaurant and then go off around the corner to gamble or watch a show."

"Is there room to add a stage?"

"If they've handed over their gelt to buy my food, then I'll let them wander off to listen to a song and a joke from the best that Hollywood can provide. It's gaming money that I want."

"You're going to put a casino inside the Nacional?"

"Why ever not, Alex? Just because it is old doesn't mean it can't bend with the times."

Meyer leaned back in their Lima Hastiada booth and surveyed the room. In the middle of the afternoon, there were only two occupied tables, and they were both far enough away for any conversation between Alex and Meyer to fall on deaf ears.

"Imagine a gaming floor overlooking the bright lights of the city at night. Tourists and high rollers will flock to the place to be seen to play in the swankiest gaming joint in town. We are going to turn the most luxurious hotel in Latin America into the greatest casino on God's earth."

"How does Batista feel about your plans?"

"He agreed to give me the gaming license yesterday, and I wired appropriate funds overseas and to the government account today. It's a done deal. As I am the minister for entertainment, how could I refuse my own request to convert some usage of the Nacional over to gambling?"

A grin ripped across Lansky's face—this was why he had spent those years schmoozing with Batista while everybody else focused on Vegas. Meyer's vision was so much broader than Benny's in building an entertainment capital out of nothing.

"Meyer, how can I help?"

TWO WEEKS LATER, Alex met a fella at the airport from times gone by—Gus Greenbaum from Las Vegas. Along with his sidekick Moe

Sedway, Gus had taken over the Flamingo Hotel the day after Benny was whacked. That showed how much both Meyer and the Italian members of the syndicate trusted him—the previous owner had not been careful enough with their money.

"Good to see you again, Gus. How's Vegas?"

"All is fine, thank you. Massimo sends his regards."

"Pleased to hear it. We are going to be working together in Havana."

"Really? Meyer led me to believe I'd be on my own, Alex."

"You are running the Nacional project, for sure, but Meyer has asked if I can work alongside you to iron out any local difficulties you may have."

"Are we expecting any?"

"Not yet, but you never know what will happen and if a problem were to appear, then I will make it go away."

"You always were good at solving problems, that's why Benny brought you into Vegas."

"Something like that, Gus."

GUS DIDN'T TAKE long to place a call with Alex and ask for a private conversation, so they met in the Lima Hastiada that afternoon.

"Is the food any good here?"

"Passable, Gus. I've tasted worse."

Greenberg ordered a sandwich and beer, while Alex only took a refill on his coffee and a pile of tortilla chips to nibble.

"How's the Nacional going?"

"Fits and starts, Alex. At the moment, we have some issues with a union."

"I thought we'd driven them all out of town."

"Not so's I've noticed. We are gutting the floor which has gone all right, but now the plasterers, carpenters, and electricians are refusing to work unless we up their pay rate."

"And that's not in the business plan?"

"Nope and Meyer has been very clear to me we cannot go over-budget on this project."

"That's what happens when you work for penny-pinching Jews."

"Tell me about it. I've been employed by them all my life and look where it's got me."

The two men chuckled before Alex focused on the problem at hand.

"Are you sure there's a union involved?"

"No, but their action is orchestrated. I mean, they've all asked for the same amount of gelt and they did it yesterday, every last one of them."

"And there's no wiggle room on their pay?"

"Not a red cent, unless we get the go-ahead from Meyer. If I add to my costs here, then I'll have to cut corners somewhere else, and we both remember what happened at the Flamingo when Benny did that."

"Let me have a word with them and we'll see what happens."

LUCIO RUIZ SAT opposite Alex in the bar at the Nacional. Two beers stood between them. Lucio had downed most of his, and Alex hadn't taken a single mouthful from the glass nearest him.

"How does it feel sitting front of house in this place, Lucio?"

"I could grow used to this life, Mr. Cohen."

"Call me Alex. Yes, physical comfort is worth paying a premium for, wouldn't you say?"

"If you can afford it, Alex, then you are right."

"How did you get the job here to work on the casino project?"

"A friend of a friend, you know how these things operate."

"Lucio, I don't. I am not a builder, but a businessman. When somebody wants me to do a job, he comes up to me, straight up, and asks me to my face."

"Well, that's not how contracts are here, senor."

Alex detected a hint of sarcasm in Ruiz's voice in the last word he uttered. He let it go but didn't forget it either.

"I hear there has been an impasse in the project. An argument over money has stopped the work. You know anything about that?"

"Alex, with all due respect, you know that's the case otherwise I wouldn't be having a drink with you in the bar of the Nacional Hotel. I'd be lucky to be allowed through the front entrance of this joint."

"Lucio, you are right and I apologize. You should be thrown out of this place and I will happily organize that for you, if you want me to. I understand there is a hypocrisy in that you can be here when by my side and not allowed in the building in other circumstances. But you need to think beyond what's left of your beer and consider why we are seated in this booth."

Alex gave Ruiz some time to ponder over what he'd just heard, but the blank expression opposite him showed that those thirty seconds had been a waste of time.

"They have offered you and your friends a very fair wage, and yet you want more. Why is that?"

"Alex, sir, we are not fools. Once the casino is built, then Mr. Greenbaum and his business partners will make a fortune out of our efforts. So we reckon it can't hurt to ask for a few more pesos an hour because we won't see any of the profits that our toil generates."

Alex ground his molars as he had heard this sob story, or one like it, a thousand times before, and on each occasion it annoyed him.

"What you don't seem to understand is that each party takes on different risks and is paid accordingly. The proprietors must pay the staff, heat the building, buy food, and so on hoping guests will stay in the hotel and spend their evenings playing roulette or cards. All those costs have to happen before one customer steps through the threshold. The owners take on that risk."

Alex paused for a second for Ruiz to absorb this information.

"On the other hand, you are being given money to do something short term. You are paid after you have done your work and this is taking place in President Batista's hotel, so you know you will get your money at the end of the week."

Another pause.

"Of course, Lucio, I am not pretending that you have no risks at all. For example, there can be an accident with a hammer or saw. You could fall out of a window and come crashing to the ground. You might find that your family is injured in their home, or worse. Your body could be found in a shallow grave on the beach or thrown overboard a boat in the bay. All these things could happen and some of those risks can be removed."

Ruiz's face was ashen now, and he had stopped pawing his glass with his muscular hands.

"What do I need to do so that my family shall be safe?"

"Go to work at the rate of pay that has been offered to you. If you don't do this, then you can be certain that some harm will befall you. I don't know when or where, but you, your wife, and your children will be in mortal danger."

Ruiz swallowed hard and licked his lips.

"Gus Greenbaum and I worked together in Las Vegas a while back. Ask around about me in case you don't believe my words. I am going to go now. I haven't touched my drink so you are welcome to stay and have the second beer. Then you should leave and come back to work first thing tomorrow morning. If you do, all will be fine and you shall have gained two Nacional beers inside you."

"And if I don't?"

Alex rose and smiled. Then he walked to the bar to settle the check and left Lucio Ruiz to consider whether he should knock back the beer or get out while he still had breath in his body.

MAY 1958

31

"I'D LIKE YOU to hit someone in Havana."

Alex stirred his coffee while maintaining eye contact with Vito Genovese, who had paid the island yet another of his brief visits. He had flown in that morning on his private plane and was scheduled to depart before sunset.

"Talk me through the situation and I will see what I can do, Vito."

"Sam Giancana and his Chicago friends need their wings clipped and you are the man for the job."

"I appreciate you thinking of me, but I don't want to stand in the middle of any Italian beef. With all due respect, one of the pleasant aspects of living in Cuba is that I do not get embroiled in local disagreements back home. As we both know, the syndicate has faded away and I would have thought the commission was more than capable of handling these sorts of matters without involving outsiders."

"Alex, my friend, you are right that the syndicate has withered on the vine and that we Italians look after our own. But Sam has overstepped the mark and needs to face the consequences of his actions."

"That may well be, Vito, and I am not making any judgment as I am in possession of no facts. This remains an Italian American problem, surely."

"Are you concerned about repercussions?"

"I will not insult your intelligence. Meyer and myself do work with many, and often competing, outfits over here. If I assist you in this matter, then my neutrality may be broken and I'll endure the negative consequences of my decision—either through loss of revenue or someone will take a hit out on me. I do not wish to live in a world where there is a vendetta against me. The safety of my family is too important to allow business to threaten their lives."

Vito's eyes bored into Alex, arms folded and lips pursed. He could see the Italian's muscles twitching in his cheeks. He unfolded his hands and lit a cigarette before responding.

"Alex, we both know you have been instrumental in several high-profile hits over the years. You are too much of a professional to confirm this but Albert Anastasia, Benny Siegel, and Abe Reles are the first three names that come to mind—all dead and buried because of you and I respect you for your work."

"I don't know what you mean."

Vito raised a hand to stop Alex in his tracks.

"And even here in front of me, you continue your denial: bravo. But these men are in their graves and you walk free, so let's not pretend too much, eh?"

Alex shrugged and cast his eyes down at their table in the private meeting room in the Nacional that Meyer had provided for their conversation. The waiters had left a pot of coffee and some food before Alex had dismissed them and Vito had arrived.

"Do you fancy a bite to eat, Vito? I'm going to grab a sandwich even if you are not."

Without waiting for an answer, Alex walked over and piled salt beef on rye onto his plate. Then he refilled his coffee and returned to his seat.

WHILE THEY ATE, Vito refrained from talking business with Alex and the fellas covered topics like the state of gaming in Vegas and prostitution in New York and Chicago.

"Alex, you have avoided answering my question for long enough."

"Earlier you said that Sam's actions needed consequences. While it is none of my business, I would appreciate you telling me what has warranted you wanting him dead."

"I thought the whole point of a Murder Corporation hit was that you asked no questions about the contract."

"Vito, this isn't a Murder Corp deal though, and the fact you have come to me indicates that the contract hasn't been sanctioned by your commission."

He eyed Vito's response to this suggestion because the Italians had kept to their own ever since the syndicate evaporated from view. Suddenly, the fella had flown more than a thousand miles to spend an afternoon with Alex to get him to whack one of their own. There was something queer about this request.

"You understand my role in the commission's hierarchy?"

"Vito, of course I do, and I congratulate you on your coronation, which should have happened at Apalachin but was delayed a few weeks. And I respect you and the position you hold. Like Charlie Lucky before you, I applaud good things happening to great men."

Alex raised his coffee cup as if he were clinking a beer glass.

"But this is not personal. Even if Luciano were to walk into this joint and ask me to do the same thing, I would want to know why I was the lucky one to be chosen for the task. I am a businessman nowadays. I operate and manage several hotel services across Havana. The days of plugging men for cash are behind me."

"Alex, I have come all this way to ask you especially. This should speak volumes about how important I view this situation and the request I am making of you. That should be sufficient answer to any of your questions."

"It is, and it isn't, Vito, and I have listened to what you have said and mean you no disrespect when I press you on this. But the fact you have come here means this is not a commission-sanctioned contract and that can leave me open to reprisals."

"If you are only doing my bidding, then you have nothing to fear from the others."

"Vito, that may well be the case today and tomorrow, but at some point in the future, you may no longer be the boss of bosses and I might still be alive. Then I shall not be under your protection over this murder and bullets will fly aimed straight at my heart."

The Italian opened his mouth but said nothing—as though this was the first time he had considered the assassination of Sam Giancana from anyone's perspective but his own.

"I will pay you handsomely."

"Vito, there is no doubt that the fee would be significant, whoever gets to pull the trigger, but this is not some clever ruse by me to increase my pay. I am not negotiating with you, because were I to do so then you would believe I was prepared to carry out the hit."

"The other thing you should consider, Alex, is whether you wish to turn me into an enemy. After all, this is the first time I have asked you for any sort of accommodation and you intend to refuse my request."

"Please don't put words in my mouth, Vito. And I do not want us to part on poor terms today, no matter what conclusion we reach on your proposal. If you have heard half of what I said, then you will understand the reasons for my desire to pass on it and free you to find somebody else to fulfill the contract. I hope you respect my decision in light of my reasons and that we can still do business together. For example, at present, there are several million dollars a month we launder for you through our hotels and I imagine you would like us to continue to carry on with that, even if Sam continues to breathe well into next year."

Now it was Vito's turn to take the heat out of the conversation and wander off to the side table to refill his coffee and grab another sandwich. He stood and ate while keeping his eyes trained on Alex. After a mouthful of coffee to wash the rye flavor away, Genovese returned to his chair opposite Alex.

"Is there nothing I can do to change your mind?"

"Vito, ten years ago I would have agreed immediately and there would have been no conversation, but I am older now and my family has drawn towards me for all my faults. So this isn't about what I want as much as it is about what is best for them. Agreeing to this hit can only do them harm in the long term, so I must decline with regret and respect."

Vito stared at Alex for five intense seconds, then he blinked, as though he was snapping out of a trance, and lit a cigarette. He inhaled half without uttering a word, flicking ash off the end. Then he stood up.

"Alex, thank you for taking the time to see me today. I must return to New York and make other arrangements. I cannot pretend to be happy with the outcome, but I respect your decision and understand why you are refusing to do this job for me."

"Vito…"

Before Alex could respond, Genovese walked out of the room and into his waiting limousine. Alex called the airport an hour later to confirm that the fella had left the island. If Alex hadn't been concerned with ensuring the safety of Sarah and his boys, then Sam Giancana would have been sleeping with the fishes before the end of the week.

32

ON THE OTHER side of the island, the rebels had been quiet for several months and Alex wondered if they were about to break cover. Batista must have had the same thought because he called in Meyer and Alex to ask them to head over and survey the scene. Like before, this meant Alex and Ezra found themselves sat in a tent opposite Captain Izzy Chávez.

"Have you had much contact with the rebels?"

"Nothing in the last two months. Most weeks, they'll attack a police vehicle or my soldiers on reconnaissance, but there hasn't even been a sound out of them."

"That is peculiar. Any ideas, Ezra?"

"I'm blank. It suggests they are cooking something up though. Izzy, were there any thefts of munitions or arms before they went into radio silence?"

"No major hauls from around here, but that doesn't mean they couldn't ship them in from another part of the island. These barracks are not the only place to get rifles in Cuba."

He was right. Either the rebels had packed and gone home or they were about to descend from the hills and reap merry havoc on the town. The chances were they hadn't given up and returned to their jobs in the fields.

◆ ◆ ◆

THE ANSWER FROM the rebels came two days later, before Alex and Ezra got back to Havana. They stayed in the Moncada Barracks as Izzy couldn't guarantee their safety if they boarded in town, and regretted that decision shortly before nightfall.

Alex heard a whizz over his head and he recognized the sound from his time in the trenches back in the fields of France. He shouted, "Mortar!" just as the first one landed twenty feet away from his tent. The boom as the missile hit the ground shook through Alex's chest and a plume of soil showered on the canvas. He hit the dirt with his hands covering his skull, like he had received his basic army training only the other day, instead of forty years before.

Screaming and shouting engulfed the air space as the soldiers responded to the attack. Alex popped his head out of the tent and first turned to his left to check on Ezra, but there was no sign of him.

"You in your tent, Ezra?"

"Sure thing, and I ain't coming out until this is over."

Alex took in all that he could see. Men rushed up and down the aisles in between the rows of tents and at the end of the row, a group stood firing indiscriminately into the tree line, but there was nothing to indicate that was where the rebels were situated.

He dashed over to Ezra's entrance and scurried inside.

"It's only mortar. They want us to stay still so we are sitting ducks for them. Trust me and make a break for it. My bet is that they're scaring us but do not want to engage with this army. Izzy is a good enough soldier to have trained these men well."

"Where do you think we should go?"

"To a point of safety. Follow me and stay close."

Out of the tent and away from the trees, Ezra trailed Alex as he wended his way along past the tents to the permanent huts. These barracks were only meant as a temporary measure to keep military control of the southern part of the island when Batista seized power so a few buildings with corrugated iron for walls had been put up and everyone and everything else had to make do with canvas tents. The mess was too important a location and was the first to be erected as a permanent structure—it needed running water to function well too.

They ran past the mess and noticed some troops lying on the floor inside, as though that would stop a mortar from landing on their heads. Then past more tents, enough for a platoon and beyond that… dunes.

The barracks were situated smack on the edge of the island, and Alex figured that heading for the beach would offer them the best protection. Over the ridges and Alex took a quick look at the tide—it was going out so there would be a vast expanse of empty sand if they went far enough and plenty of time to remain there before the sea lapped at their ankles.

Ezra got the idea and pointed at an upturned hunk of wood. When they drew close, Alex saw it was a boat with a massive hole in it. Terrible for sailing but great as cover in case the rebels swarmed the camp and came leaping over the hill.

The mortar fire continued for another twenty minutes, but it was all aimed at the barracks and not at the beach. When everything had quietened down, Alex and Ezra tentatively picked their way back to the camp to see what damage the rebels had inflicted.

"MEYER, THIS WAS not a good sign. The rebels had the entire barracks pinned down by only three or four of their men. We shouldn't underestimate them."

"One well-planned attack doesn't mean that Batista is going to be deposed. I spoke with him yesterday—they call themselves revolutionaries, but they are just a bunch of disgruntled farmers with the Castro brothers leading them around the hills like sheep."

"Those lambs nearly blew my head clean off, Meyer."

Alex's friend looked at him as though he was a foolish little boy.

"I think Batista's iron grip remains on the throat of this land. Those rebels might have made a big noise down south, but the actual onslaught takes place in the city every day of the year. The secret police abduct miscreant citizens at night and they are never seen again. The papers don't report it, and their families are too scared to even talk about it among strangers. That's the real crisis in this country, Alex."

"Meyer, I had no idea you were so concerned about the ordinary joe in the street."

"We live together, we love together, Alex. Everybody must look after their own. Let the saps living here do what they want; all that matters to me is that we can build Las Vegas in the sun."

"Are you more interested in creating something bigger than we dreamed was possible in Nevada or making money?"

"Alex, to do one, you must do the other, as far as I'm concerned. The important thing is that nobody must stand in my way. I don't care who they are or how powerful they might be, Havana is where I shall make my mark."

That night, Alex told Sarah about his conversation and asked her what she thought about Meyer.

"The fella has an amazing vision. A gambling haven in Latin America. If he could pull that off…"

"That's the question, though. Do you think he will?"

"The man is the minister for entertainment, has the ear of the president and you for his muscle. How can he lose?"

"Sarah, I've seen Castro's rebels first hand—those guys mean business. There may not be many of them, but they would give any gang member in Little Italy a run for their money."

"Are you saying we should leave Cuba?"

"No, at least I don't think so. Not right now, I mean. But I believe Meyer underestimates them and that might cost us dearly."

"Alex, is it safe to have David here?"

"Yes, for the moment. If I thought it wasn't all right for David, then you'd need to leave too, Sarah."

"Do you want me to go, Alex?"

"I never want us to be apart, but if this place gets dangerous, for whatever reason, then, of course, I'll need you back in the States."

"Now you're getting me worried."

"Don't be, Sarah. At the first sign of trouble, we'll all be out of here. I've left everything behind me before and I'll do it again, although that's not my plan for Havana."

"You would say, though?"

"Sarah, you have my word."

DECEMBER 1958

33

MEYER GOT WHAT Meyer demanded and the new wing of the Nacional Hotel was set for its first paying customers before Christmas, or as Lansky preferred to comment, "I knew you guys would get it ready before Hanukkah."

The Casino Nacional was positioned next to the Starlight Terrace Bar and the Casino Parisién night club. They were located so that the clientele would have the shortest distance to travel to flit between gaming, booze, a show, and more gaming. Paradise on earth only a hundred miles from Florida.

Gus had been good to his word and brought the project in on time and under budget, in part thanks to the persuasive skills of Alex, who convinced the workers to take a pay cut in exchange for their families' lives around Halloween when they seemed to be slacking for no good reason that anyone could make out.

Opening night at the Nacional passed without incident. Meyer had made it low key because all he was interested in were the high rollers who would appear as soon as they took the covers off the poker tables. The tourist trade would pick up as quickly as word got out back home that a new venue was open for business and Lansky didn't need to spend any money advertising that fact; the travel agents would do all the work for him.

Although Alex had half-thought he'd bump into Townsend again, he was glad he didn't have to put on a monkey suit for the night. The days of dressing to impress had long since faded in his mind, and he preferred to spend the evening with Sarah and David rather than making small talk with a bunch of strangers. He was getting old.

Instead, Alex remained in the bar and restaurant to save himself from falling foul of the dress code in the casino. The lack of publicity didn't prevent Meyer's friends and partners from coming to town to celebrate the launch, and so it was that Vito Genovese appeared that evening and plonked himself next to Alex, who ordered them both a Scotch.

"So we meet again, Vito. How's business?"

"All good, Alex, thank you for asking."

"Are you over here for the grand launch?"

"I always like to see new places opening up to allow more people to be separated from their hard-earned cash."

"Meyer will do well here, Vito."

"Let's hope so. And how's tricks with you, Alex?"

"Good. There's plenty to keep me busy and, as you said, there's a lot of money to be made in this town."

"From what I've heard, Meyer is the sole owner of this gambling establishment."

"That's what I reckon. The man wants to create Las Vegas in Cuba —one casino at a time."

"A fella with vision. How very old school. The rest of us Mustache Petes just want to make money, launder it and then spend what's left on our mistresses and maybe our wives now and again."

Alex smiled but had no interest in being drawn into a conversation about extramarital affairs. He hadn't strayed from Sarah since they'd got back together after Rebecca's death. He had a flash of Ida's face beneath a pillow as she struggled to breathe before her body slumped still.

"Alex, are you interested in having more money than you currently make?"

"That's a rigged question. Have you ever met anyone who is satisfied with their lot?"

"Not in America."

"So, what proposition do you have for me this time, Vito?"

"All these American tourists you're going to gather at the Nacional, walk in with clean cash and leave poor."

"That's the plan."

"I guess at some point the dollars you accept at the counters get put into bags and deposited in a bank which then wires the money back to the US."

"Vito, you don't have to warm me up. Cut to the chase, please."

"As you know, I have the utmost respect for both you and Meyer and all that you have achieved together over the years, not least what you have done on this island. I would like to launder money from the mainland through the Nacional on an exclusive basis."

"I assume you have a monthly minimum figure in your head."

"We are talking ballpark a million a year."

Alex whistled. That was more than chump change.

"I am glad business is going so well for you."

"Thank you, but what do you say?"

"Vito, this isn't my call. Meyer owns the joint, and he decides who he does business with, not me. You've asked the wrong fella."

"I understand the situation, but you must admit I stand a better chance of getting an exclusive deal with Meyer if you are backing it."

"Sure, but why not just launder the money through here, even if others are doing the same?"

"Meyer Lansky might not be the Big Bankroll, but he is the next best thing. My only criticism is that he acts like a bee, buzzing from one flower to the next. I want him to hover over my plant and give it some special attention."

"Let me think it over. When do you intend to approach Meyer over this?"

"The day after tomorrow. This might be a great place to make money, but there's too much Spanish spoken for my taste and I need to get back home."

"WHY WOULD I want my hands tied behind my back, Alex?"

Lansky and Alex were talking the following afternoon in Meyer's penthouse.

"That's not for me to say, Meyer. The fella came to me with a business proposition, which I am relaying to you. It's your casino and you decide who you deal with, of course."

"Genovese should have come direct to me, then I would have had the chance to tell him what I think of his proposal."

"Meyer, perhaps that's why he swung by me first. But let's be straight. I do not wish to be an intermediary, standing in between you two. If you can't talk directly with each other on this, then I want no piece of it."

Meyer left his armchair and paced up and down in front of Alex, who relaxed into his seat, knowing this was going to be a long ride. After a couple of minutes, Meyer stopped in his tracks and lit a cigarette. Then he returned to his chair.

"Feeling better after your promenade, Meyer?"

"There's no need to be like that. Vito annoyed me with his entire approach. Since when does the fella need an envoy?"

"When he's Italian and doesn't want to lose face if you reject him."

"Alex, that man and I go way back; I funded his first heroin smuggling operation before the war."

"He was a young Turk back then. Roll forward twenty years and Vito has a lot to lose nowadays and is generating over a million a year in cash he has yet to launder. The fella has picked you to do the job, not some Italian from his old neighborhood."

"That's why I don't want him using the Nacional."

"Meyer, I don't get your point."

"All my life I have wanted something to call my own. Since I was a kid, I have been fantastic at lending money to fellas who pay me back—and some. Great, but these joints in Havana are the first opportunity I've had to construct some action for myself from the ground up. This is mine and nobody else's."

"With a little help from the president."

"I told myself when Batista took control that I wanted this to be my *shtetl*—my town, my home—and there shouldn't be Italian money funding it."

Alex thought for a moment, mulling over what he'd heard.

"Hasn't that ship sailed decades ago, Meyer? You've done business with the Italians since the days of Arnold Rothstein and

Charlie Lucky. They expect you to maintain that relationship even when you are abroad. You've been swimming with the sharks too long to complain they are in your self-declared inlet."

"Alex, I don't want to use the Nacional Hotel to launder Italian money. This is going to be the basis of all my new ventures, including The Panama. *Yiddishe gelt.*"

"I'd be surprised if Vito sees it like that. He will take it as a snub."

"I'll offer him better terms to handle his cash through a different joint."

"Meyer, is it only about the money? Do you think Vito is testing you in some way?"

"Huh?"

"Has he ever asked for an exclusive contract before?"

"Alex, no—not that I recall."

"Then why now? Why you and why here?"

Meyer blinked twice and stared at Alex as he sipped his coffee.

"What do you reckon, Alex?"

"I'm not sure, but the Feds are snapping at the Italian mob's heels and they can now trace the movements of cash like never before. In Cuba, we are beyond the FBI's jurisdiction and Hoover needs some wins to show he can hit the commission hard. If I were Vito, I'd want to ensure I had at least some of my eggs in a different basket. Wouldn't you?"

"Does that mean we can count on him?"

"He is the head of the Italian's commission—the boss of bosses. Of course, you can't trust him. He'd slit your throat as soon as look at you if you stopped being of any use to him. Same as all the Italian bosses—they never invited us to Apalachin, remember?"

34

"I GAVE YOU until the end of the year to sign the Panama contract and here we are in December, Alex. Are you going to piss or get off the pot?"

Lansky might have carried a smile on his face, but his tone was cold—like an impatient teacher talking to a kid who doesn't do as he is told. Alex shifted in the booth at the rear of the Lima Hastiada. Meyer had asked to meet him here rather than in his suite, which sounded off, but Alex paid no attention to it.

"Meyer, David has prepared the paperwork, so this isn't a kiss-off, but I have some reservations about the deal."

"Is that you speaking or your son?"

"David provides me with legal advice and I decide. If you are annoyed with me, please don't drag other people into the conversation."

Meyer sighed.

"What's your concern then, Alex?"

"It is a question of risk and reward. While I have never pretended to you what I think of Batista, I can suck that in if the results are worth it. I am a realist, Meyer, and I know that when you swim in the sea, there are always sharks surrounding you. But I do not want to hand over a million to that man if he will not be running this country."

"Alex, the guy has an iron fist that smashes all opposition."

"Not quite, Meyer. You're forgetting about the rebels. Batista might have total control in Havana, but that's just not true on the other side of the island. You should visit Moncada Barracks and you'd see what I mean."

"I don't need to travel to the other end of Cuba to recognize that the rebels are a small band of nobodies stirring up trouble with no popular support. The Castro brothers are nothing to worry about. Your money will be safe."

"Meyer, it is more than my money that is at stake, it is the future of my family. If I invest in The Panama then the financial security of Sarah and our children rest in the bricks and mortar of one entertainment complex..."

"Which will make more money than you and yours could spend, Alex. There might not be certainties in this world, but you can bet your last cent on The Panama turning a profit within months and generating enough gelt in a year than you have ever had in your life."

"Above what I make out of Vegas?"

"You get ten percent of the skim there and that's nothing to sniff at, but that's chicken feed compared to one hundred percent of a place like The Panama."

"I wish it was that simple, Meyer."

"But it is, Alex. You are overthinking an easy question: do you want to make enough money so that you could retire with Sarah wherever you wanted. No more and no less."

Alex wondered what was really stopping him from signing. Perhaps Meyer was right—wire the money over to Batista today and by the end of the week he'd have a gaming license in the bag and in six months, the hotel would be open and this time next year, he would be in clover. What's not to like?

"David tells me there is too much risk on my side. Batista's name is absent from the agreement and he is the party with the most influence over the outcome of the deal."

"Alex, some things are better done on trust than in any paperwork, and Batista's word is only as good as his deeds. Naming him in a contract would be a futile gesture and would gain you nothing but tsoris. It would annoy him and make him difficult to deal with in the future. Nothing more."

"That makes Batista sound like a cranky child, and that's the guy you want me to do business with?"

Another steely look by Meyer.

"I have been working with that petulant child for years now with no problems. Does he have an over-inflated sense of his own importance? Sure thing. Does that stop me from making money through him? Nope. Nothing is simple when there's gelt involved."

"Meyer, it's not like I think the whole matter is a bad idea. If I did then we wouldn't be having this conversation as I'd have nixed it a long time ago…"

"Great, Alex, so wire the money over and stop grousing."

"But as you so rightly say, nothing is simple when there's hard cash at stake. I want to be clear about the risks involved. For me to fund the venture without having to go cap in hand to the Italians for fundraising, I'm going to have to put everything I own on this horse. If the deal goes south, then I will be left with nothing. *Nothing*."

Alex emphasized the last two syllables to get Meyer to think outside of his admiration for Batista. The slimeball was as keen as Lansky to create Las Vegas in the Caribbean, and their interests had been entwined ever since the Havana conference when Benny's fate was sealed. That was over a decade ago, and Meyer had made significant sums of money out of that generalissimo.

Lansky paused for a second, and Alex wondered if he had got through to his old friend.

"I've told you before, you don't have to go to any outside parties for funding. If you want financing I am happy to offer it to you at more than reasonable rates. I hope that serves as a powerful indicator that I want you on board with The Panama and that I am prepared to back you with my own money in order to secure your involvement. We don't need the Italians because they have made it clear they do not think they need us anymore."

"Charlie has long gone, for sure, Meyer."

"And our future is in this island. Three or four years from now, our legacy will be complete."

"Your legacy, Meyer. I'm only concerned to look after my family."

"In years to come, they'll remember both our names in Havana like the older fellas recall Benny in Vegas, only we won't be skimming the take and getting our girlfriend to fly overseas with the money."

THIRTY MINUTES LATER, Alex thought he had turned the conversation away from The Panama, but Meyer had other plans.

"So is there anything else you need to know from me before you wire the payment to get your gaming license, Alex?"

"How tight are you with Batista?"

"What do you mean, Alex?"

"You're his minister for entertainment and you bought into the Nacional before any of us had even heard of Cuba. Yet there you were going into business with a man who was about to lose an election."

"Alex, I trust Batista enough that he will look after me, but only when our interests are aligned. We both like to make money and while the gelt rolls in, I know I am safe with him and he'll do right by me. But I am not naïve—the day the casinos stop creating wealth is the time I need to leave this island or ask you to fulfill a contract on the guy."

"Meyer, how long do you think you will both board the same gravy train?"

"Business is cyclical. When they banned liquor, we thought bootlegging would last forever, but it didn't. Same here—eventually we will run out of space to build new casinos or there'll be no more tourists to fly over here. At that point, we'll max out and takings will plateau. Sometime around then, I will need to separate my investment interests from Batista. That is many years away though."

Alex pondered Meyer's words. He wanted it all to make sense, but he was aware of a gnawing at the pit of his stomach. If this gamble of his went south, the Cohens wouldn't have a penny to rub together.

"Has David been whispering in your ear, Alex? Is this why you can't commit?"

"We both know my son has had issues with the wording of several of the clauses, and that's all been ironed out between him and you. I don't have a head for paperwork so when he tells me the contract's good enough then I believe him. For me, a handshake is all I ever need. As you've said yourself, a business relationship is all about trust and not much else."

A sip of coffee each and just as Alex opened his mouth to continue, Meyer held up a palm.

"There we have it, Alex. We are all about faith. If you can't trust me enough to invest in The Panama, then I can't trust you to work with me in Cuba and you should go home. Give me your signature on the bottom of the contract by the time the banks open after the holidays or pack your bags and leave."

DECEMBER 31, 1958

35

THE NEW YEAR'S Eve ball at the Nacional de Cuba was the swankiest event in the Havana calendar where Batista hosted a lavish dinner and dance for all his friends, senior government officials, and his extended family. Meyer, Alex, Sarah, and David were honored to be on the top table, albeit ten seats away from the man himself.

Alex surveyed the ballroom and wondered how many people it contained—the sea of bobbing heads seemed to go on forever. For a second, he remembered the times he had spent at Arnold Rothstein's New Year celebrations. Sarah nudged him in the side to push him out of his reverie.

"How many of these people do you know, Alex?"

"Sarah, there's the four of us, the president and his brother. The rest are total strangers or I recognize them and have nodded or smiled at them since we arrived in Havana."

She giggled.

"I'm glad it's not just me then."

"These are Meyer's guys, not mine. I tolerate Batista and his cronies because we can make money here; the man is a disgrace to his uniform."

Sarah's smile evaporated, and she squeezed his hand.

"You do what you have to do. We live together, we love together. Right?"

"And we die alone. Maybe we'll hang on for a couple more years, produce a big pot of gelt, and head home. What do you say?"

"Is that your way of telling me you've signed the papers for The Panama?"

Before Alex could reply, the trumpets from the band screeched into a rumba and all words were lost beneath the cacophony.

"SURE FEELS GOOD, doesn't it, Pop?"

David's face was lit up with enthusiasm for the coming year, buoyed by the copious amounts of champagne poured down his neck by the waiting staff. No expense was being spared, and the lawyer hadn't even got to the end of the soup course.

The rectangular head table ran across the ballroom and all the others spread like tentacles away and down the room. Located near Alex and Meyer were Batista's Italian friends—close enough to lean backward for a short while and exchange pleasantries. Alex and Lansky looked out on the vista while Sarah and David stared at podiums with flowers perched on top of them lined along the back wall.

Alex caught Vito Genovese's eye; the man was at the nearest point on the Italians' table, and he smiled in response. They hadn't spoken since Meyer rebuffed Vito's exclusive money-laundering deal. Alex knew it was nothing personal but aimed at anyone whose family hailed from Sicily, although Genovese didn't share Meyer's perspective. Alex was lucky to get any acknowledgment of his presence at all.

Once the soup bowls were cleared away, Alex excused himself from the table and idled over to Genovese.

"Good to see you, Vito. How's business?"

"All well, thank you, Alex. It would be better if Meyer had seen sense over my proposal, but that's behind us."

"Pleased to hear it, Vito. There's plenty more deals for us to make in the future."

"Thank you for saying so. That might be true for you, but I'm not so certain you speak for Meyer on this."

"Oh, Vito. He likes you and enjoys working with you. From what I know, this is the first time since you fellas began to do business that he has ever refused a favor for you. Even then, it was done with respect and you can be sure that no one received a similar deal. Meyer wants a small piece of Havana to call his own. No more and no less."

"Interesting to hear that, Alex. I thought he snubbed me, but perhaps I shouldn't have taken it so personally. Now that's twice when you guys have refused me."

"They are serving the next course. I'd better return to my seat. Let's talk some more before the end of the night, all right?"

BEFORE HE WALKED back around the head table, Alex put his hand on Sarah's shoulder, interrupting her conversation with David. Alex leaned down and whispered in her ear. "Quite an evening. I love you." She smiled as he kissed her on the cheek, stood up, and returned to his seat opposite her.

"It has been a profitable year, Alex."

"Sure has, Meyer. Even the Nacional is showing healthy numbers and it's only been open a handful of months."

"I'm glad I didn't go into bed with Genovese over the money laundering too. This place is my piece of paradise and I don't want to share it with anyone—present company excepted."

Alex grinned and clinked glasses with his old friend. The fella had been there for him before he went upstate to Sing Sing and had looked after him ever since, one way or another.

"Meyer, what can I say? I'm sat in front of my family—people I might never have seen again if it hadn't been for you—and we are on the brink of greatness. Actually, where's your wife and kids?"

"On vacation in Florida. They'll be back next week."

"That explains why I haven't seen them for a few days... Yeah, what we will do over the next five years will make history."

A sip of champagne each and Alex chuckled.

"What's funny?"

"That we're going to do better than all those Italian gonifs over there, and they don't even know it yet. We'll be retired before they get assassinated; very few bosses survive to old age."

"Don't gloat just yet, Alex. We need the money in the bank first. Talking of which, have you wired the payment to Batista's account for your Panama gaming license?"

Another squealing roar from the trumpet section announced the end of the meal. Alex looked down to see that busboys had cleared the tables, and the guests at all the other tables were ushered away from their chairs so they could convert the space ready for the band to play so the dancing could begin. Naturally, the top table was excluded from these antics and within a handful of minutes, the musicians rose and kicked off with a toe-tapper which drew almost everyone onto the dance floor.

Before Alex could protest, Sarah grabbed him by the hand and dragged him to join her to rumba. He wasn't well-practiced but did his best not to crush her feet. She smiled and wiggled her hips to the beat. But after only one song, Alex was forced to admit defeat. He turned round and caught David's eye, beckoning him over. "Sarah, you deserve someone who knows how to do this." Then he walked off and perched next to Meyer.

Just as he inhaled to start a conversation with his friend, Vito sat down in front of them and lifted his glass. They sipped their champagne, and the Italian leaned forward.

"Another year, another dollar."

Meyer raised a smile.

"Despite our differences, I wish you a long life and every success in the coming year, Vito."

"And to you, Meyer. Although if you disrespect me a second time, I won't take it so quietly."

"I always respect you in all that you do and what you have achieved. Sometimes business partners disagree, and the strength of their partnership keeps them together. That is what you and I have, Vito. It's not just about the money, it is down to character. We are men, not boys."

Meyer glanced at Batista, who remained glued to his seat in the center of the head table. There was no way the most powerful man in

Cuba was going to be jiving on the dance floor tonight. Genovese followed Lansky's line of sight and nodded.

"Wearing a uniform doesn't make you a soldier. Isn't that right, Alex?"

"Absolutely, Vito. When you've got your hands dirty with the blood of your compatriots, that's when you are a fighting fellow."

"Gents, let's not darken the mood on this evening of celebration. To our success in the future with General Batista, the greatest man ever to wear that uniform."

With a glint in his eye, Meyer clinked glasses with Alex and Vito as they acknowledged his toast. Alex looked into the sea of couples dancing and saw Sarah and David in the heart of the throng.

As the music wound down, the bandleader took to the mike to remind everyone that it was only a minute before midnight. With that news, Sarah and David headed back to Alex, and Vito made his excuses to return to his fellas.

With ten seconds to go before the new year arrived, everybody in the room counted down... three, two, one. Happy New Year!

JANUARY 1, 1959

36

BALLOONS FELL FROM the ceiling, and everyone howled and whooped for the new year. Alex held Sarah in his arms and they kissed. "Happy New Year, my love." They hugged for an eternity and kissed again until Alex noticed someone hovering near them—David was waiting.

Sarah got to him first and hugged him, so Alex took Meyer by the hand to man-hug him, slapping his upper arm twice. Then Alex reached his hands out to David and wished him well while Sarah gave Meyer a hug and a peck on the cheek.

The band played Auld Lang Syne and everybody crossed arms and sang along until the orchestra stopped and a spotlight aimed at Batista, who had stood up to make his annual speech.

"Another year has gone by and Cuba has got stronger. The economy has grown year-on-year since the people showed their support for me when I took power. Their faith in me has been entirely justified. I stand before you all and I look to the future, filled with optimism and hope. Thanks in part to your investment of time and money in our country, I expect even better things to happen to my state. There will be greater foreign investment in the entertainment industry in Havana, and we shall benefit from the know-how provided by our American friends in the construction sector."

The president inhaled to grab what appeared to be his first breath since he began speaking and, at that moment, a guy who was dressed as a waiter scurried into view and handed Batista a scrap of paper. Then he vanished into the crowd.

The general's expression indicated he was not expecting to be interrupted, let alone by someone so menial, and he paused to read whatever was on the note he'd just received. His eyes widened, and the color left his cheeks.

"Thank you and goodnight. Enjoy the rest of the celebration."

Alex blinked, and the president had gone.

"What's going on?" asked Sarah, but Alex had no better idea than she did.

"Is this some kind of gag, Meyer?"

"Not that I know of."

Alex gazed at the faces staring at where Batista had been standing only a minute before, but he couldn't make out anything that would give a clue to what happened. All he knew was that the president had walked out on his own party.

"WHAT NOW, ALEX?"

"Not sure, Sarah. Stay near me until we figure this out."

His tone had switched to somber instruction. Despite his reassuring words, Alex was not happy. Batista's expression had contained shock and confusion, which he hadn't seen on the face of that trumped-up uniform since he arrived on the island.

Meanwhile, half the band started playing and some guests danced, unconcerned by what had just transpired. After all, it was a New Year's party—the host might have left but there was still celebrating to be done.

"What's Batista up to?"

Vito marched up to Meyer and asked a very reasonable question in an aggressive manner.

"Your guess is as good as mine, Vito."

"I thought you were part of his inner circle."

"We are close, but not so much that he tells me everything he plans on doing. Whatever it is, I'm in the dark like you. All I can advise is that we all stay sharp."

Hearing Meyer say those words, Alex regretted not bringing a revolver out with him. He had allowed himself to get soft in this city.

Although the orchestra continued to play and people danced, a quick glance at the exits showed many guests were leaving. Even members of the band were packing up their instruments and walking away. A waiter hurried past and Alex grabbed his arm for a second.

"Can we order some more drinks?"

"Get them yourself, senor."

The guy wrenched his limb out of Alex's grasp and continued on his journey across the ballroom. He felt Sarah's fingers intertwine with his, and Alex turned to discover that David was only inches away from him.

"Whatever happens, we stick together—just remember that. If you can see me then I can see you. We don't know what's going on, but we must stay near each other."

Then Lansky chimed in.

"Where's Francisco?"

"Who?"

"The brother. And Batista's wife. The entire entourage has left the building."

Alex scanned the room again and found that Meyer was right.

"What was in that note, Meyer?"

The two men hurried over to where Batista had risen during his speech. Alex hunkered down and scoured the floor, and Meyer pulled apart the party debris from the table surface. Among the cigarette ends and spilled booze, Alex's fingers came upon a scrunched-up ball.

He rose and revealed the note: *LEAVE NOW*. Alex showed it to Meyer, who was equally perplexed.

"At least we know he followed the instruction."

Alex stared at Meyer for a second.

"That's not the point. We don't know why he was advised to go and who told him."

The last of the band stopped playing and half the guests who hadn't already left the second-floor ballroom remained on the dance floor, unsure what to do or where to flee.

"Everyone stay here. Do not move. I'm just going to see what is happening outside the ballroom."

"Don't leave us, Alex."

"It'll be fine, Sarah. Trust me."

Before she could respond, Alex let slip her hand and marched toward the exit, matching the slow flow of tuxedos out into the lobby. There was a constant murmur of conversation, but nothing more than that or any sign that anything was happening beyond the confines of the Nacional.

Alex considered venturing down the broad spiral stairs but thought better of it. There was no knowing what might be round the corner, and he needed to make sure his family remained safe. As soon as that thought was planted in his head, the only thing Alex could do was scurry back to be by Sarah's side.

Yet another quick look around and Alex couldn't see Vito or any of the other Italians, which got him wondering if they had been tipped off at the same time as Batista. A squeeze of his elbow and Sarah brought him back to the here and now.

"There didn't appear to be anything happening the other side of that door, but who knows what's going on in the streets."

"Let's find out."

Meyer strode away from the top table and fussed with some red velvet drapes that formed the backdrop to the ballroom wall. He tugged at them with all his might and they opened enough to reveal a set of doors, which led onto a balcony. They followed him out to survey the Havana streets.

A GLANCE AT the world in the early hours of the new year and you'd say there were still hundreds of guys walking along the streets, but as Alex's eyes became accustomed to the darkness and the sparkling light from the stars and lampposts, he realized that most of the ants down below on the sidewalks were stationary. Those people walking along the roads were getting jeered and shouted at. This was not any party spirit Alex had seen since his arrival in Cuba. They stood tens of feet away from the action, but the tone of the voices and the body language of those they could see revealed a menace as far removed from a new year's party atmosphere as you could imagine.

Sarah gripped Alex's fingers tightly, and he felt David edge closer and put a hand on his shoulder. Meyer leaned over the balustrade, keen to hear what was being said, but the voices were too far away.

A crashing sound of splintering glass and a fireball appeared in the middle of the street. People ran in all directions, unsure of the source of the explosion or quite what was going on. Women screamed and a herd of revelers stampeded from the Nacional.

"It's time for us to leave, everybody. No good is going to befall us if we stick around in the hotel. That was a Molotov cocktail, and they rarely come on their own. If those people are as angry as they sound, we need to get as far from this joint as we can."

Sarah and David needed no further explanation, but Meyer was less certain.

"This is my hotel and I can't allow anyone to attack it."

"Meyer, this is Batista's place and the most important thing right now is to make sure we are all safe. Without that, your investment in this building will be worth nothing."

His friend thought for a moment and then nodded consent. Alex led him and his family back into the ballroom, down the stairs, and out through a side entrance marked for staff only.

37

THEY FOUND THEMSELVES in a blind alley to the side of the Nacional with dumpsters, rats, and the stink of sewage within their grasp. Alex led them toward the alleyway entrance where people rushed past. Screams. Elbows jostling. The smell of burned gasoline in the air.

There were two groups in front of them: those wearing evening dress were scurrying away from the hotel and the casino area, fear in their expressions and with good reason. The other group looked like locals and there was hate in their eyes. Some guy who hustled past the alley turned to sneer at Alex and spat in his direction before continuing on his way.

"We've all got to stay real close. There's some ugly goings-on round here and we must all be very careful."

To emphasize his words, Alex pulled off his bow tie and removed his cummerbund to make himself feel less conspicuous while wearing a tux. Meyer and David followed suit while Sarah stood and stared. Alex took her clutch bag and stuffed its contents into his pants pockets and threw the bag on the floor.

"You won't be needing that."

She widened her eyes and then nodded. Her jaw stiffened and the old Sarah returned, the one Alex had met back in the Bowery. They both knew that they would do whatever it took to survive. Sarah seized his hand and Alex led them onto the street.

◆ ◆ ◆

THEY TRIED TO act as though they were out for a stroll—on the night when the only people on the street were seeking or fleeing mayhem. As Jews, they knew how to be invisible in plain sight and did their best to march along the sidewalk with purpose while not attracting attention.

Throughout this time, Alex and Sarah remained glued to each other's hands as they wended their path down one street and up another. Alex knew exactly where he was going as he had walked the same journey countless times, albeit under calmer circumstances. Whenever they reached a road where there were too many angry locals, he'd switch left or right to keep on going but ensure they kept out of harm's way.

He reckoned they were only three blocks away from their home when he stopped to take stock. They were at a T-junction, and both the left and right streets contained large gatherings. Alex looked around and stood to his full height.

"Where are David and Meyer?"

Sarah turned around to see that the two men were no longer behind them.

"No idea. Should we go to find them?"

"Sarah, let's get you safe before we worry about the other two."

"But, Alex, which way can we go?"

She was right. They were going to have to double back to avoid the two crowds ahead, but there was no guarantee they wouldn't come across the same problem around the next corner. All Alex knew for sure was that staying still was not an option.

They strode back down the street they'd just come from, and Alex spotted a side alley between two houses. He scurried towards the gap and they entered the darkness of the passageway. Although Alex wanted to keep plowing ahead, Sarah slowed him down and he looked at her to figure out why she wasn't running at full pelt. She put a finger to her lips, and he realized she'd noticed a group marching along the sidewalk, past the alleyway entrance and off to the junction they had just been standing at.

Once they were both certain the group would not come by any time soon, Alex and Sarah hightailed it down the alley and out the other side, returning to the glare offered by the street lighting. Alex inhaled and smelled the sea.

"This strip by the coast is filled to the brim with expensive housing and foreigners. We must tread carefully."

Sarah nodded.

"What if they've fire-bombed the house?"

"Let's worry about that later. We've got to get there first."

Although he was right, Sarah didn't appear satisfied with the answer. If they'd burned the place to the ground, then there was no point fighting their way around the crowds to get to it.

"Where to now then, Alex?"

He looked up and down the street—nothing. So they headed back north toward the sea and nearer to their home. Just as they reached the corner to turn left, they stopped in their tracks. Fifty feet in front of them was a gang of thirty or forty men, clubs, bottles, and rifles in hand. The ones nearest them glanced back, saw the couple, and nudged their friends. Even if they bolted for it, they had been seen and there was no way they could outrun thirty guys. They were trapped.

ALEX KNEW BETTER than to reason with a group that large and instead, inched slowly backward and whispered, "Follow my lead, Sarah. No sudden moves to spook those guys and don't make a break for it unless I do it first. If so, do your best to get back to the house, whatever it takes. We'll wait for each other there."

"Got it."

While facing the group, Alex carried on taking a pace or two backward then stopping, all the while ensuring he remained with the front of his torso pointing in the mob's direction. He figured in the darkness, they would find it harder to judge distance and so might not notice the gap between the couple and the group was widening.

They had reversed almost to the corner of the two streets before one of the group nudged his friend and stepped forward.

"What are you doing, senor?"

A machete dangled from one of his hands, practically scraping the floor. Alex stayed silent and moved back one more pace; there were twenty feet between them and the man. The guy took two steps toward them and tilted his head, trying to see who this couple were. Alex noticed there was a streetlight just behind, which meant they appeared as silhouettes to all the people who stood before them.

Alex's Spanish wasn't good enough for him to sound like a local and he didn't want to alert the group that they were within feet of a pair of foreigners, so he ignored the guy's question and took another pace back, along with Sarah.

Loreto Melendez took several steps toward them again and Alex saw his face, the anger in his eyes directed at them, even though they had done nothing to him and his compadres.

"Why don't you answer my question?"

This time the guy spoke in English and there was an edge to his voice. One of his friends stepped forward and shouted out for him to sort out these two strangers. He nodded and jogged forward, blade raised to his shoulder.

When he was ten feet away from Alex, Melendez brandished the machete above head height and Alex let go of Sarah's hand and pushed her away from him to the side. Loreto upped his pace and ran at Alex, swinging the blade straight at his head.

One quick sidestep and the machete swung down and missed Alex by a foot; he grabbed at the guy's downward-plunging wrist with one hand, catching him unawares because of his speed, Alex used his other palm to reach out to Melendez's face or neck. He didn't care what he snatched at as long as it hurt.

Sure enough, Alex's fingers wrapped around Melendez's collar and he squeezed the throat hard. Loreto dropped the enormous blade in response to losing his breath and grabbed at Alex's hand on his windpipe. He kicked at one leg and Melendez overbalanced and fell with a thud onto the concrete road. All the while, Alex held on and landed on top of him, plunging his fingers deeper into Loreto's larynx. With no threat from the machete, Alex put both hands on Melendez's neck and pulled his head up, only to slam it onto the hard surface of the street. Once. Twice. Three times and the body went limp beneath him. Sarah exhaled with a hiss as she recoiled from the murder she'd just witnessed.

Alex looked up and saw her staring at him. Then he shifted his head to check on the rest of the huddle of men. He grabbed for the nearby machete and got to his feet in time for two more guys to step forward. They hung back because the glint of Alex's blade made them extremely aware that he was armed, and he'd already shown them he was dangerous.

"Whatever happens, you must get yourself somewhere safe, Sarah. Do you understand me?"

"Yes, but…"

Alex stood to his full height and waited.

"When I count to three, you are going to run back down the street. I will be right behind you but don't turn around because that'll only slow you down. And be as fast as you can."

He inhaled so he'd know she could hear him under his breath.

"One. Two. Three. Go!"

38

SARAH'S FOOTSTEPS RECEDED into the distance and Alex held his ground, wielding the large blade for all to see. Someone from the crowd lunged forward but Alex clipped his shoulder with the machete. The guy tumbled down, clutching his upper arm, and screaming in pain. The others near the front tried to take a step back —they had not been expecting one of these foreigners to put up much of a fight, but they hadn't encountered Alex before.

"Leave us alone. We've done nothing to you people. Let us pass by in peace and you won't have to suffer the consequences."

He was outnumbered thirty to one, but Alex's chief concern was to buy Sarah enough time to escape from this mob. He waved the machete some more as another guy edged forward from the group, weighing up his chances of getting the better of Alex. He was a little younger than the rest.

"Don't even think of trying it, boy. That is your last warning."

This sufficed to goad the boy into action and Alex knew it. Before the runt got within five feet of him, Alex swiped with the deadly blade and a blood-curdling noise emitted from the kid as he fell to the ground with his hands around his throat but he only had seconds to live as Alex had deftly slashed him from ear to ear. A murmur rose from the gang. They wanted revenge but didn't want to die.

Alex swallowed and focused on taking some deep breaths. He wasn't as young as he used to be, and he recognized the fear in the pit of his stomach. They were hanging back for now, but groups of angry men only wanted blood and he needed to time his next move precisely.

He swung the blade over his head so everyone could see it and as the machete entered the downward phase of its motion, Alex rotated round using the momentum of the knife and hit the sidewalk hard with his right foot. Then he ran as fast as he could away from the mob and down the street. Three seconds later there was a roar of noise as the men chased him, screaming abuse, their boots and shoes thumping on the concrete.

Alex didn't look back because he had the sound of their feet to judge how close they were, and his advice to Sarah was right—it would slow him down. He had one advantage over the mob; he knew where he was going and headed through the alleyway which was narrow enough for him to be sure that it would slow a group that big down a little.

Out the other side and then a choice: left or right. He and Sarah had come from the right and so he went left, hoping that the trouble they'd fled earlier hadn't moved further on. The sound of boots on the ground grew noticeably louder and Alex allowed himself a peek behind. Most of the men had reached the end of the alley but he had gained fifty, maybe one hundred, feet on them.

Alex kept on pelting along the sidewalk, looking for another alleyway or some other way to gain ground on the guys baying for his blood. The answer came in the form of a building in the middle of the street. Just a glance at it and Alex knew nobody was home—the broken glass for windows, the hanging piece of wood for a front door. Its other advantage was that there was no gap on either side. He ran at the entrance, kicked the door off its hinges, and scampered into the house.

WITHOUT HESITATING FOR a second, Alex sprinted through the entrance hall and entered the kitchen, which was strewn with boxes, rats, and who knew what else. In the darkness, Alex bashed into a waist-high cupboard and ricocheted off other unknown furniture until he got to the back door. Then out into the yard and he stopped.

There was fencing all the way round with a gate to the right. Alex pulled the exit open and considered going through it, but halted. By the wall to the left of the kitchen was an outhouse with tall grass and weeds in front.

Alex sprinted over to the outbuilding and took his shoulder to its door, which fell open easily enough, and he closed it behind him. He bent down with one eye peering through the crack in the gnarled wood and waited. Twenty seconds later a horde of men spewed into the yard and the first out of the kitchen staggered and headed through the gate. With the initial three out of the yard, the others followed until there was nobody left of the swarm and their noise subsided.

Alex waited for a count to sixty and then he peeked out: nobody. He skedaddled through the house and out the front, careful not to bump into the mob in case it had doubled back on him. With nobody on the street and nothing to see, he headed back to the alleyway and zigzagged to his home.

There were no lights on inside and he gulped. He opened the door and stepped into the entrance hall. "Sarah!" A body lunged at him, arms engulfed him, and Sarah kissed him hard on the lips. He needed no light to recognize the person hugging him for dear life. She was safe, and Alex allowed a tear of relief to trickle down his cheek.

"WHY NO LIGHTS?"

"There've been hordes running past, and we figured it would be safer if they didn't know we were here."

"We? Are Meyer and David with you?"

"No, Alex. There's only Ezra."

Now that Alex's eyes had got used to the darkness again, he noticed a figure standing in the doorway to the living room. He walked over and shook the man's hand.

"Good to see you are all right, my friend. Where did you get to this evening?"

"After midnight, I tried to make my way to the Nacional, but there were too many people on the street with hate in their hearts. So I figured I'd head straight over here and wait for you to appear; it had to happen at some point."

Alex walked past Ezra and slumped down on a couch, his legs buckling under him, he had been fleeing for so long. Sarah sat next to him and Ezra kept a watchful eye on the scene outside on the street. She brought him a glass of water and Alex relaxed for a minute to regain some much-needed energy.

"No sign of David or Meyer?"

"None."

The sadness in Sarah's voice tugged at his heartstrings, and Alex focused on the problem at hand.

"We can just wait for them to show or go and try to find them. Ezra has done the waiting for us, so I'll grab a gun and go back outside to look for them."

"You can't do that, Alex."

"We have no choice, Sarah. The sooner we get David back in one piece, then the sooner we leave this city."

"Let me go with you."

"No, Ezra, as much as I'd like your help, you have the more important job of staying here and protecting Sarah if any trouble should come calling. Understand?"

Ezra looked unhappy, but Alex knew his lieutenant would follow his instructions until the day he died. Alex knocked back the rest of his water and fumbled around his study until he had a revolver and four boxes of ammo. Then he dashed into the bedroom and changed into ordinary clothes.

He shoved the pistol into his pants pocket and kept the machete at hand. Sarah kissed him and flung her arms around his neck, not wanting to let go.

"Let me leave, Sarah. That way I will be back before you know it."

"Bring him home alive."

He brushed her cheek with the backs of two fingers before picking up the blade and heading out the door.

"If I'm not back in an hour, grab whatever you can and head to the airport. Do whatever you need to do to get off this island."

ALEX'S FIRST MOVE was to return to the Nacional and figure out quite where they'd lost David and Meyer in their rush to leave the area. This proved a short-lived plan as the streets were heaving with people, shouting and smashing any store window selling American goods. After a few minutes' thought, Alex realized he was going about this the wrong way, He was wasting his time attempting to retrace their steps. What he must do was think like Meyer and decide what he'd do if he was separated from the rest and needed to hide out somewhere safe.

Before long, Alex had skirted around the Nacional to the other side of the hotel, away from the coastline, and hopped from sidewalk to sidewalk until he reached the Lima Hastiada. Its frontage was boarded up, almost as though the owner knew there was trouble ahead, so Alex scampered to the rear to see if there was an open window.

All the windows were a no-show, but his luck was in, the back door was ajar instead. He took out his pistol and entered, listening for any sign of life. He edged into a room filled with crates of wine and tequila, as well as cases of beer. There were various kinds of food on a set of tall shelves to his left.

Alex shuffled to the door that led from this glorified store cupboard and into the private meeting area at the rear of the cantina; his usual booth was ten feet away from where he stood. He pressed his ear to the intervening door before slowly turning the handle and allowing it to creak open. He clenched his teeth, inhaled a lungful of air, and pushed the door wide enough to walk into the main bar.

Alex hit the dirt as he heard the click of a hammer being drawn back on a gun. One slug whizzed past his ear in the semi-darkness— the sun was rising outside. As much as Alex wanted to shoot at the person or persons unknown, he hadn't seen from which direction the bullet had come. Four boxes of ammo would soon become none if he sprayed the room indiscriminately.

"We've got the place surrounded," he lied in an authoritative tone. "Cease firing and everyone will get out of here alive."

There was a heartbeat, and then a timid voice broke the eerie silence.

"Pop?"

"Yes. Is Meyer with you?"

"Who else would've taken a shot at you? Not your *fercockte* son, that's for sure."

39

BACK AT ALEX'S home, everybody huddled in the living room in the dawn's half light. They'd closed the shutters on all the front-facing windows. Alex and Sarah sat next to each other, while Meyer and David were in two armchairs. Ezra stood by the door, always with one eye on the main entrance.

"Meyer, I think I understand Batista's note."

"No kidding, Alex."

"Is he still on the island?"

"If I know Batista, he'd have gone straight to the airport and off to the States before we'd inhaled after he exited the ballroom."

"Wouldn't he need to grab his gelt?

"Sarah, he holds almost all his money in private banks in Switzerland and Bermuda. The little he had lying around would've only kept him in chump change for a week."

"Meyer, his spare cash is what most of the men in Cuba call a lifetime's wages."

"That may be so, Alex, but this is no time for a discussion on Cuban politics."

"I wasn't planning on it but you admit that if he'd treated his people better, then maybe they might not have chased him out of the country."

Lansky looked down at the ground, watching his dream of a Vegas in Cuba slip through the floorboards.

"What'll happen if the rebels take over?"

"First thing I'd guess is that Meyer will no longer be minister for entertainment. You've lost that job, my friend."

Meyer continued to stare at the ground and didn't respond.

"Then there'll be a few changes—for the people, by the people. Based on what I saw last night, the guys on the street were destroying American stores. We won't be flavor of the month."

"Alex, what shall we do?"

"Sarah, first we need a better idea of what the hell is going on beyond the confines of this house. Second, we need to get ready to leave. Whatever is happening, I don't think we will be welcome at the minute, at least not until some of the heat dies down. Ezra, I need you to stay here while I go out. Will you need to grab any of your things when I return?"

"I'll live without any clothes I'm not wearing. Looks like I won't be saying goodbye to my girlfriend."

"Write her a letter when we are back in the US. Sarah, pack everything that's important into two suitcases. Anything we can afford to leave behind, then we will. David, do you need to get anything?"

"I have some papers…"

"If they are to do with business dealings in Cuba, forget about it. The regime after Batista can't possibly operate on the same terms as the generalissimo."

Sarah walked upstairs and David went to the kitchen to search for coffee for everybody. Meyer remained where he was, unaware of the bustle surrounding him. Alex sauntered over and squatted in front of him, placing a hand on his knee.

"Meyer, I need you to get it together. With Batista gone, all our leverage has flown out on the same plane. We must be ready to leave. You need to work out if there is anything you have that wasn't on the top floor of the Nacional because there is no way on earth that you'll walk inside that building again."

His friend looked up and stared straight ahead.

"Meyer, I'm going to check out what is happening on the streets and then we shall figure out how to get off this island."

JUST BEFORE HE left the house, Alex tied a handkerchief over his face to shield his less than Hispanic features. The streets in this affluent area were vacant; last night's violence had given way to this morning's calm. He kept to the shadows and did his best to travel behind the houses rather than on the streets to hide from any potential trouble.

Eventually, Alex arrived near the center of Havana, a thousand feet from the casino district, and that is where he found the good people of this fine city. They were marching or listening to men making impromptu speeches about how everything was going to be better now that they had driven the evil Batista out of Cuba.

Alex smiled beneath his mask. Ordinary folk like the ones gathered in front of him never had it any better. People with money make more money and that was how it had always been.

Restaurants and bars had opened up hoping to catch some trade from thirsty and hungry rioters. This contrasted with the broken glass and empty stores where the signage indicated they aimed the contents at American tourists. Alex thought about the Lima Hastiada and decided that it was worth a visit.

Using the same caution as when he'd come into town, Alex sidled his way over to the cantina to see if it was open. Sure enough, there were barflies at the counter and two occupied tables. He headed straight for his back booth and waited. The owner came over and asked him what he wanted.

"Some information and a drink, if you'll serve me."

"You got money? Then I'll bring you a coffee. Anything else and I'm not so sure."

"Just tell me what happened last night. I know Batista fled, but why then?"

"Haven't you listened to the radio, Alex?"

"If I had, would I need to ask you?"

"The rebels took Santa Clara yesterday. Word is that they are now marching on Havana."

"How long do you think it'll take them to get here?"

"Less than a week. The twenty-sixth of July Movement was never a big band, but with victory in the south and Batista out of the way, their numbers will swell."

"So my family and I have time to breathe?"

"Some gasps maybe, but you don't want to be here when Castro arrives in town. The man has spent the last three years making speeches about how all the problems of Cuba are down to Batista and his capitalist cronies. With all due respect, Alex, I think he was talking about you."

THE REBELS MIGHT be a day or two away from Havana, but that didn't make the place any safer for Alex, his family, and friends. The best course of action was to get out that day because who knew what would happen tomorrow.

"We can try to catch a seat on the ferry to Key West or head for the airport."

Alex summarized their options when he got back to the house. Lansky appeared not to have moved the entire time Alex was away, and two cases were stuffed to within an inch of their lives by the door.

"I have a twin-prop."

Meyer broke his silence and dropped a simple piece of information in their laps.

"A private plane at the airport?"

"Yes, of course. When you are in Batista's government, they are one of the perks of the job."

"Is it yours or Batista's?"

"That doesn't matter right now, Alex. We have a means of leaving the island with no customs officer in the States getting his nose put out of joint wherever we land."

"You have nothing with you, Meyer. So why do you care about Uncle Sam?"

"Not now, but I need to empty some safe deposit boxes before I go."

"Meyer, I wasn't planning on taking anything like that. Isn't it more important that we are alive? We can always make more gelt somewhere else."

Meyer sighed.

"To make gelt, you need gelt and, in America, I was always careful not to have any asset in my name—for tax reasons, you understand."

Alex stared at him, not comprehending the implication that Meyer thought so obvious.

"This means that most of my wealth is in gold and cash. I can't get it wired anyway because there are no records that I own it. I am the only one with a key to the deposit boxes. If I don't leave with the money, then I'll have nothing."

"What about your income from your other investments?"

"I put it all into Cuba. This was to be my paradise."

Meyer sank back into silence. Alex's mind raced. They had no idea how long the airport would remain open, assuming flights were still being allowed right now. And the longer they waited to allow Meyer to grab his loot, the more dangerous it could be. The innkeeper believed it would be a few days before the rebels hit town but Alex knew more than him about how armies behaved. He reckoned they'd arrive tomorrow, if not later that day.

Right now there was a vacuum at the center of power in the capital and Castro couldn't afford for anybody like another tinpot army general to seize the moment and take over before the rebels arrived.

40

"THIS IS THE deal, everyone. We'll drive over to the airport or as close as we can get. Then into Meyer's plane and away we go. All of us—not one person will be left behind."

Nods all round and Ezra opened the door and scurried to Alex's car to bring it from where it was parked at the back of the house. With still nothing on the street, they packed the trunk with cases and piled inside, Alex and Ezra at the front and the other three in the rear.

For most of the journey to the airport, there was nobody on the streets and no trouble along the way. The situation altered as they approached the outskirts of the airfield fencing. An armed guard stood at the first entrance and the barrier was down. Alex didn't fancy convincing a bunch of yokels to let him through, so he kept on down the road.

Alex turned right, and the vehicle headed north until they reached another barrier surrounded by a second crew of rebels. He slowed the saloon down and stopped two hundred feet short.

"Keep sharp, Ezra. Let's stay calm but prepare for the worst."

Alex trundled the car forwards and halted in front of the roadblock. One of the group, toting a rifle with the barrel resting on his arm, indicated for him to stop even as he hit the brake. Alex wound down his window.

"Afternoon, what is your business here?"

"We wish to buy tickets to fly out and are hoping we can get away today."

"Where are you intending to travel to?"

"The Bahamas."

"Are you Americans?"

"Yes, we have been working over here and now we want to leave. What's going on in your country means that we won't be able to earn a living until things calm down."

"What do you guys do?"

"We're involved in the entertainment industry."

"I understand why you're wanting to get out of here, but we cannot allow you to do that."

"Can you explain why please?"

"We are restricting the number of flights out of Cuba, and the only individuals allowed into the airport compound already have tickets."

Alex nodded and took another look at the group. There were four, two behind the guy who'd done the talking and one on the other side of the vehicle near to Ezra. Alex tapped on the shift stick to get Ezra's attention and gesticulated his intentions.

"My friend is just going to help me turn the car around, okay?"

"If you don't know how to drive, what's a guy to do. Go ahead but make it quick."

Alex smiled and attempted to imply some humility by not looking straight into the guy's eyes. Ezra hopped out and headed for the barrier while Alex returned the vehicle to the road and then executed a poor reversing maneuver so that Ezra was forced to slam his palm against the back of the car to stop Alex hitting the obstacle. Meanwhile, the crew laughed at Alex's bad driving and chatted to each other, making jokes at his expense. He didn't mind.

The turn signals flipped on and the windshield wipers flashed left and right at high speed before the engine stalled. Alex shook his head and stepped out of the car.

"Sure isn't my day. You got a light?"

Hector Sastre, the chief, laughed at him and fumbled around his pockets until he found a book of matches. Alex took a smoke from his pack and leaned towards him, cupping the end of his cigarette to stop the wind from attacking the fire that appeared in front of him.

As he shifted position to bend down and avail himself of the flickering flame, Alex dropped the cigarette and whipped out his pistol, putting a slug in the center of the leader's stomach. His body recoiled slightly, but Alex grabbed his neck and swung round to face two more of the group. With Hector to shield him, Alex twisted and poked the barrel of his gun under the guy's armpit.

Two clean shots and the men's corpses twitched on the ground. Another shot rang out and Alex looked over. Ezra stood over the last body and kicked it to make sure the guy was dead. They raised the barrier and Alex turned the engine over. Then they thundered inside, following the single-track road until it reached an open space with hangars all around.

"Where's your plane, Meyer?"

"Hangar sixteen."

"And what about the pilot?"

"Good question."

The enormous numbers painted on each hangar let Alex know where to go. Within sixty seconds, they were inside the building and Alex pondered their next move.

"EZRA, DO YOU know how to fly a plane?"

"You're joking, right, Alex?"

"We need someone, don't we?"

Ezra looked around just in case a pilot might appear inside the hangar, but no joy.

"Any suggestions, Meyer?"

"Next door is a rest area away from the customers. We might find one in there."

That was the best idea they had, so Alex stashed his gun and strode through a side entrance that Meyer pointed at. Inside were several tables and chairs, along with some couches and armchairs, the sort of environment a pilot would use to relax in between flights or to catch a nap.

Only trouble was that the place seemed deserted and the sheer number of half-empty cups and glasses showed there had been quite an exodus. Alex walked through an open door on the other side of the space into a room with some beds in it. Sure enough, this was where pilots came to sleep.

Just as Alex was about to leave the suite, an enormous sound erupted from nowhere. On closer inspection, the noise emanated from a man in the far corner whose head was hidden by his sheets. Alex pulled out his gun and aimed it at the guy as he threw off the bedding.

Another snore was the only response, so Alex tapped his chest with the tip of the revolver. An eye opened and then Mike Sniders sat bolt upright.

"Easy, my friend."

Sniders stared at the barrel of the gun and remained still.

"Where is everybody and why didn't you join them?"

"No idea. I've been out cold since the early hours of this morning. I ferried a guy off the island and came back because he said his friends would be over later today."

"Are you from the US?"

"Sure am."

Alex picked up the guy's jacket from the floor and read his identity badge.

"Mike, this country is no place for Americans right now. The rebels are moving in on Havana and when they do, they are going to be more concerned with the lives of the local population than with the likes of you and me."

Sniders stared some more at the gun, and Alex lowered it to help him keep Mike's attention on the matter at hand.

"You prepared to fly a group to the States? We'll pay you a decent rate."

"I said I'd wait for this other bunch."

Alex raised his pistol so Mike could get a good look at it again.

"There's money in it for you and you can still come back and pick up more passengers. We've got a plane for you to use, but we need to leave now. What's your answer?"

"Cash and a plane?"

"Yep. And keep the aircraft once we're done with it. That's got to be worth something to you."

Sniders thought for two seconds and then agreed.

"When are we going?"

"As soon as you're ready for takeoff."

MIKE TOOK A couple of minutes to get himself together and hustled about the kitchenette to make and consume a mug of coffee, all the while watched over by Alex. Then into the hangar where Sarah and David nestled next to each other and Meyer stared blankly into nowhere. Ezra's gun was in his hand; he stood by the entrance permanently on the lookout for trouble.

Sniders entered the ten-seater and Alex followed him just in case he got clever. But the most he did was switch on the engines and check the fuel.

"Someone was here before. You rarely leave a plane lying around with a full tank."

"I'd guess that Batista's planes had different rules."

"Are you telling me we're about to steal an airplane from the government?"

"That's the old management, Mike. The general won't need this jalopy again, he's already fled the country."

"In that case, I'm ready as soon as you guys hop on board."

Alex exited the twin-prop to speak to the others.

"It's time to get on the plane and Mike will take you out of here."

Sarah looked at him quizzically.

"You're coming too, Alex?"

"I'll pay Mike for a return trip and he can bring me tomorrow. If we have any hope of salvaging anything, we must act now but you guys need to be safe on American soil."

"If you stay, then so will I."

"Sarah, this isn't a debate. I need you to get on that plane and make sure David gets back in one piece."

"Alex, gelt is never worth the trouble you take over it."

"I've stashed enough money around this city to keep us in clover if I can get at it all before the rebels arrive."

He hugged her tightly and whispered in her ear. "But I need you to leave now. We'll see each other tomorrow. I promise."

They kissed and Alex led Sarah onto the plane, followed by David and Meyer. Just before Ezra stepped onto the airstairs, Alex caught his arm. "Look after them for me. If Sniders causes you any trouble, kill him when you get on the ground." Ezra nodded and boarded the twin-prop. Alex entered the cockpit and sat down in the copilot's seat.

"Mike, this is the deal. I'll pay you two hundred and fifty dollars to fly my family and friends to the Bahamas. And five thousand in total to come straight back and pick me up here."

Sniders whistled. That was what he'd normally earn in a year, and Alex hoped this would swing the deal.

"You're not coming with?"

"I've got some loose ends to tie up, but I want to leave this hellhole tonight and you're the man to help me."

"How d'you know I won't welch on the deal?"

"You only get paid when I see you again."

Alex beamed at Mike and the guy mulled over the proposition for four seconds until he agreed. They shook hands and Alex hopped off the plane and helped Mike to close the door. Then he stepped back as the aircraft taxied out of the hangar and waited for permission to take off. With no other planes on the wing, Alex watched his family depart Cuba in less than a minute. Now he needed to scoop up as much of his money hidden around Havana as he could before Sniders returned and Castro's men waltzed into town.

41

THE GOOD NEWS was that Alex had access to any tool he might need as the maintenance crews had departed as quickly as anybody else from the airport site. He figured that if the rebels were protecting the boundary fence, then they intended to seize control of the runway as soon as they entered Havana. He used metal cutters to create a hole in the mesh fencing so he could get back in with no permission from anyone at a barrier.

Mike would take a little over an hour to reach the Bahamas, have the inevitable mug of coffee, and return after another hour so Alex needed to ensure he was at hangar sixteen in two hours. This would not be sufficient time to get the job done. A glance at his watch and he made some calculations.

Sniders would need to accept an overnight layover if Alex was to reach all the places he needed to in the city. Until Castro's forces arrived in the vicinity, Mike would not be bothered. No one would be stupid enough to land in Havana today, and the handful of people who could get past the guards at the gates would fly off in their private planes; scheduled flights were off the agenda for the foreseeable future. Revolutions mess with capitalist timetables.

ALEX ONLY HAD about thirty minutes near the city center before having to get back to hangar sixteen to await Sniders' return. Almost three hours after his departure, a plane landed and taxied over. The engines cut and Mike appeared, grinning, along with another man. Alex put a hand on his pistol. This was not part of the agreement, although Mike might not have been as dumb as he looked. If this was a hijacking, then they'd die for their troubles.

"Hi, Alex."

Lansky's voice softened Alex's mood in an instant and he ran over to his old friend.

"What are you doing here, Meyer? Are Sarah and David all right?"

"They are safely holed up in a suite at a hotel. With Mike coming back to collect you, I thought I'd join him and pick up a few things I didn't get a chance to grab earlier today."

There was a light in Meyer's eyes that had been absent from the minute Batista left the Nacional ballroom. Alex smiled, then he turned his attention to Sniders.

"Mike, there's a slight change in the plan. The city is difficult to travel around, which means Meyer and I will need more time to gather our possessions."

"Are you about to tell me we aren't shipping out until tomorrow?"

"You read my mind, Mike."

The pilot looked down and then scanned the far distance of the airport as though he could see Castro's men marching toward them.

"That's not what I signed up to, Alex. And every minute we are here, those rebels are closing in on us."

Alex let him stew for a few seconds.

"I'll double your fee. Ten big ones to go next door to sleep and then fly out tomorrow morning."

Mike held out his hand, and they shook. Alex had known the promise of more cash would help Sniders make the right decision. The only risk was that he and Lansky would need to leave him alone, and anything could happen to him then. Most likely, he'd catch a yellow streak down his back and decide to quit the country without them.

◆ ◆ ◆

ALEX DROVE MEYER to the outskirts of the city and then hid the car in an alley. There was no point risking the vehicle being found, and they had a wide variety of locations to reach before the morning.

"Meyer, do you have any cash in the banks or is all your money in deposit boxes?"

"Are banks even open today? It's New Year's Day, after all. And yes, there's some hidden around the city."

With all his focus on escape, Alex had forgotten that this was a public holiday and that the banks were closed.

"You're right. We can forget about bank accounts unless you want us to pull a robbery this evening?"

"Alex, I figure that'd be overreaching. I just need to go round a few government buildings and apartments with a jimmy. Then I'll be ready to leave this town."

"I think we should hide out somewhere when night falls. The mood on the street only darkens when the sun goes down."

They used the next half hour to plan a route for the remainder of the day. Alex had an idea where they could rest their heads.

The number of people on the streets increased and when they got near the principal government offices, Alex and Meyer found swathes of men milling around the buildings. This meant at least it was easy to get inside the Ministry of Industry and Commerce, which was where Meyer's office had been located.

The two men walked through the main entrance surrounded by a steady stream of locals. At first glance, you'd be forgiven for thinking this was just another day, but the knives and occasional rifles slung over shoulders belied the fact that the Cuban rebels were beating a march over to the capital.

Meyer led the way up three flights of stairs and right, along a corridor, then left and into an anteroom that Alex recognized. There was nobody in the vicinity, so Alex stood guard while Meyer went inside to rip up floorboards and came out with two cases stuffed with dollar bills. Alex took one look at his friend and slapped his forehead.

"Meyer, we didn't think through the size of our stash. By the time we visit one more place, we'll have our hands full and even a stupid peasant will figure out that something's amiss."

"Let's make our way to the car, perhaps we must risk taking it round the city."

Alex wasn't happy with that suggestion. Keeping it hidden meant they wouldn't need to worry about getting back to the plane. Driving around town with Castro's army on their heels was not a great option, but it was the best they had. By the time they returned to the car, the sun had almost vanished below the horizon.

"Let's hole up for the night."

"Shouldn't we go to check on Mike?"

"Meyer, either he's flown off without us or he is asleep next door to the hangar. We can't do anything about it right now. Tomorrow we must be as quick as we can and sort out our affairs at the earliest possible moment. To do that, we need to be nearby when we wake up and I've got the perfect place where we'll be welcomed with open arms and given a warm bed and hot food too."

ALEX TOOK MEYER to the Plaza del Vapor where even on the day of Cuba's revolution, women stood on street corners seeking men with money to burn. While the fellas had controlled casinos and hotels in the country, prostitution in Havana had remained a local affair with one madam ruling the roost, just round the rear of the Shanghai Theater. Benita Rodríguez greeted Alex and Lansky as they entered her establishment.

"How are you, Alex?"

"Just fine under the circumstances. My friend and I are hoping you might have a room for us for one night."

"Of course you do, and you've come to the right place. These are trying times, but you are welcome here any day of the week, you know that."

Benita supplied girls to all the hotels that Alex looked after and they had made a lot of money together over the years.

"And if you have some bread and coffee, then that'd be wonderful."

"We can do better than that for you, Alex."

She left them in the reception area where at least a dozen women stood, sat, or reclined in various states of undress. Alex chose an armchair and Meyer reclined opposite on a chaise longue. As soon as they eased themselves into their seating, Alex felt a hand rifling through his hair and a girl in a corset and not much else flopped onto his lap.

"Thanks, but we are just browsing."

She shrugged, pecked him on the cheek, and sauntered to the other end of the room to giggle with her girlfriend. Meyer flicked his hand at an arm that had appeared on his chest, which disappeared. They were probably the only men ever to refuse the sexual advances of the nafkas in this boudoir.

Within an hour, they had eaten a fine meal with Benita, away from the working girls, and she had allocated them a room each.

"Would you like some company for the night—on the house?"

"Very kind, but we won't take advantage of your hospitality any more than we need to. All we ask is that you get one of the girls to wake us at five. We've a busy day tomorrow and want to start as early as we can."

"Consider it done."

As soon as Alex's head landed on the lavender-scented pillow, a wave of tiredness hit and he went straight to sleep.

January 2, 1959

42

ALEX AWOKE WHEN he felt someone's fingers inside his pants and he sat bolt upright. A nafka in a negligee squatted on his bed, attempting to get his attention—she'd succeeded.

"Thanks, but you've done your job."

He pulled out a couple of notes, removed her hand from his clothing, and placed the money in her palm. A smile and he pointed at the door. Alex waited in the reception area for Meyer to appear—he needed more time to rouse himself. No sooner had he walked into the room than Alex stood up and they exited the brothel, although he left a cash donation in Benita's hands, despite her protestations.

For the next four hours, they drove around the city while either Alex or Meyer popped into a building or alleyway and grabbed a case hidden under floorboards or in a wall. Although he didn't have time to count, Alex estimated he'd gathered at least two million dollars of his own gelt in the vehicle.

Meyer arrived back from a crash pad he'd kept for his girlfriend and threw a bag into the trunk.

"I have so many happy memories of that place."

Alex held a finger to his lips and Lansky stopped speaking. Something didn't feel right, and Alex couldn't quite say what it was. A low rumble in the distance; he felt it in his chest more than he heard it with his ears.

"It's time to go."

Meyer didn't need to be told twice. Alex gunned the car down the street and around the edge of town. The vehicle screeched to a halt as Alex stared along the straight avenue leading out of the city. All he could see was not much more than a speck of dust on the horizon.

"The rebels are on their way."

For a second, Alex did a calculation based on where they were, the direction of the army, and the location of the plane. Then he gulped.

"They'll get to the airport before we do."

Alex looked at Meyer.

"You'll be proved right if we stay here. What are you waiting for, you meshuggener mensch? Drive!"

Alex's foot slammed on the gas pedal and the vehicle skidded forwards. While he couldn't work out the exact speed of the rebels, the airfield seemed an awfully long way away. He gunned the car along the main avenue which led to the airport. All the while the ball of dust got larger as they headed straight towards it, hoping to reach the plane before the revolutionaries.

Ten minutes of hard driving and the engine screamed as Alex tried to squeeze every drop of speed out of the saloon. They were a quarter of a mile from Alex's hidden entrance, and the army was less than half a mile in front. A solitary vehicle sped ahead of the main group—they'd been spotted.

"Hang on tight."

Fifteen seconds later, Alex slammed his automobile through the wire-mesh fence and carried on hurtling to hangar sixteen. As they reached the entrance, Alex saw a jeep appear from the makeshift entrance and head straight toward them.

Alex hooted three times to warn Mike of their arrival. The car screeched to a halt as close as Alex could take it beside the airplane. Its propellers were already turning and as soon as he got out of the vehicle, Alex felt the airflow caused by the blades. Meyer and Alex grabbed as many cases as they could and chucked them inside the cabin. Then again, and for a third time. A glance showed the jeep five hundred feet away.

"Meyer, get in. There's no more time."

His friend shook his head and went back for a fourth set of bags. Alex grabbed him by the arm and slapped him on the cheek.

"We're dead if we don't leave now."

A bullet flew past their heads as if to emphasize Alex's point. Meyer blinked and ran to the airplane door. Alex took out his gun and fired a meaningless shot in the jeep's direction which was only two hundred feet away. As soon as Alex was inside the plane, Mike taxied forward.

"Get us up, Mike, as quick as you can."

Alex aimed at the jeep's tires but missed due to the abrupt movement of the twin-prop as it trundled onto the runway. A hail of bullets came from the rebel vehicle, but none touched the plane's fuselage. The rear wheels left the ground and Alex held his pistol steady in his hands as he tried to fire off one last round. He hit the windshield, and the jeep swerved to a stop.

Then a change in the sound as the plane wheels stopped making contact with the ground. Meyer helped Alex close the door, and they sat down in the nearest seats and waited for Mike to take them to the safety of the Bahamas.

WHEN THEY LANDED a little under two hours later, the two men offloaded their cases into a waiting car that Meyer had hired for the week. They gave Mike his money and shook him by the hand, then Lansky drove them to Nassau and the Providence Hotel. Up to the top floor and into Sarah's arms. Then a hug for David and Alex flopped onto a couch.

The next thing he knew, he opened his eyes and found himself in bed. A glance at the bedside clock told him it was the middle of the afternoon, but he had no memory of how he'd got there. The bedroom door creaked and Sarah's head appeared. She smiled when she saw he was awake.

"Are you all right, Sarah?"

"For sure, now that I have you back."

"Those few hours were a long hustle."

"So Meyer was saying, especially your overnight stay."

Alex's cheeks felt red hot and Sarah grinned at him.

"What goes on in Cuba stays in Cuba, Alex."

"I can't speak for Meyer, but nothing happened at Benita's apart from a meal and a *shloof.*"

Another grin stretched across Sarah's face as she threw her dress onto the floor and wriggled beneath the sheets.

"I believe you, but you'd better work damn hard to convince me you shouldn't sleep in the car tonight."

THE FOLLOWING MORNING everybody met in the Providence restaurant. Alex ordered his usual huge breakfast, and the rest took a selection of bread, cheese, and Danish pastries. A variety of juices and coffee appeared on the table too.

"What are we going to do now?"

"Sarah, I think we should stay here for a few days and have a vacation while we figure out our next steps."

"I can't speak for you guys, but I'm staying in the Bahamas."

"Why, Meyer?"

"Because with the seed capital I rescued from Havana, I'm going to turn this place into the new Las Vegas."

Alex almost spat the coffee out of his mouth.

"Are you serious? After everything we've just been through?"

"This can be paradise on earth for us, Alex."

"Don't involve me, Meyer. I want to get back to American soil. Florida, maybe."

"You think? This is a tremendous opportunity."

Alex turned to David.

"What's your advice?"

"Pop, you didn't listen to me the last time, so why are you going to hear a word I say on this occasion?"

"Who told you that? I never wired the money over to Batista for the Panama Hotel. That's why Meyer wants my gelt now."

Meyer nodded sanguinely.

"It was never a trust issue with me, Meyer. Or rather I'd work with you until the end of my days, but I couldn't trust Batista further than I could spit."

"The offer to invest in the Bahamas is still there if you change your mind, Alex."

"Thank you, Meyer. But right now, I think I'm going to head for Florida and try out retirement. Those collections we made in Havana have to be good for something."

Sarah held Alex's hand.

"I thought you'd work until the day you died?"

"When I said retire, I meant drop a dime to Sam Giancana to see if there's any action I could get involved with."

"Alex, you tread careful with those Italians. You didn't trust Batista, but I feel the same way about Genovese, Giancana, and the rest of them fellas."

"Don't worry, Meyer. With Sarah and David by my side, what could possibly go wrong?"

THANK YOU FOR READING!

Get a free novella

Building a relationship with my readers is the very best thing about writing. I send weekly newsletters with details of new releases, special offers and other bits of news relating to my novels.

And if you sign up to the mailing list I'll send you a copy of the Alex Cohen prequel, The Broska Bruiser. Just go to www.leob.ws/signup and we'll take it from there.

Enjoy this book? You can make a difference

Reviews are the most powerful tools in my arsenal when it comes to getting attention for my books. Much as I'd like to, I don't have the financial muscle of a New York publisher. I can't take out full page ads or put posters on the subway. (Not yet, anyway).

But I do have something much more powerful and effective than that, and it's something that those publishers would kill to get their hands on.

A committed and loyal bunch of readers.

Honest reviews of my books help bring them to the attention of other readers.

If you've enjoyed this book I shall be very grateful if you would spend just five minutes leaving a review (it can be as short as you like) on the book's page. You can jump right to the page by clicking www.books2read.com/heel.

Thank you very much.

Leo

SNEAK PREVIEW

In Book 6, Hollywood Bilker…

"Thanks for taking the time to see me, Santo."

The Italian boss of Florida state nodded his acknowledgment of Alex's words as they sipped their coffees in the back of one of the many casinos owned by the Sicilian in Miami-Dade county.

"Cuba was a terrible business for us all. I am only glad we were able to get out with our lives."

"Santo, I don't think I ever saw Batista travel faster than his last minutes in power. That man knew the right time to flee."

"And he left the rest of us high and dry."

Now Alex nodded as he recalled his last two days in Havana, with his close friend and business associate, Meyer Lansky, as he attempted to salvage the gelt he had secreted around the city. Alex never trusted the banks.

"That was the past, Santo. Despite all that has happened, I am trying to focus on future opportunities."

"Spoken like a true entrepreneur. How can I help?"

"I am hoping you'll make an introduction for me with Frank DeSimone out in Los Angeles."

"What's wrong with the Eastern Seaboard?"

"Nothing at all—I'd just like to get as far away from Cuba as I can, at least for a short while. Having spent so many years in Vegas and Havana hotel complexes, I thought I might check out life in Hollywood. I've mixed with another of the celebrities to know what they are like and I can see some business opportunities for myself—subject to Frank's approval, of course."

"Alex, I will happily give you the introduction you seek—you have proven yourself in the past and I wish you every success in your new enterprise."

The two men shook hands and Alex left the back room, knowing that by the time he made contact with DeSimone, Santo would have put in a good word. What Alex failed to realize was that as a former syndicate member and the fella who still ran Las Vegas, his reputation was the only calling card that he needed.

Perhaps his seven years spent in Cuba helping Meyer build a Vegas in paradise had left Alex tarnished. Certainly, the four weeks since his return to the US had given him no indication that he was anything more than a guy sitting on over two million bucks he had brought back to the country.

To grab your copy, go to www.leob.ws/heel.

OTHER BOOKS BY THE AUTHOR

Alex Cohen

The Bowery Slugger (Book 1)
East Side Hustler (Book 2)
Midtown Huckster (Book 3)
Alex Cohen Books 1-3
Casino Chiseler (Book 4)
Cuban Heel (Book 5)
Hollywood Bilker (Book 6)
The Mensch (Book 7–Due 2021)
Alex Cohen Books 4-7 (Due 2022)

Stand Alone

The Case

The Lagotti Family

The Heist (Book 1)
The Getaway (Book 2)
Powder (Book 3)
Mama's Gone (Book 4)
The Lagotti Family Complete Collection (Books 1-4)

All books are available from www.leob.ws and all major eBook and paperback sales platforms.

ABOUT THE AUTHOR

Leopold Borstinski is an independent author whose past careers have included financial journalism, business management of financial software companies, consulting and product sales and marketing, as well as teaching.

There is nothing he likes better so he does as much nothing as he possibly can. He has travelled extensively in Europe and the US and has visited Asia on several occasions. Leopold holds a Philosophy degree and tries not to drop it too often.

He lives near London and is married with one wife, one child and no pets.

Find out more at LeopoldBorstinski.com.